SKIN TAKER

SKIN TAKER

MICHELLE PAVER

ZEPHYR

an imprint of Head of Zeus

This is a Zephyr book, first published in the UK in 2021
by Head of Zeus Ltd
This paperback edition first published in 2021
by Head of Zeus Ltd

975312468

A catalogue record for this book is available from the British Library.

ISBN (PB): 9781789542424
ISBN (E): 9781789542431

Typeset by Ed Pickford

Printed and bound in Great Britain by
CPI Group (UK) Ltd, Croydon CR0 4YY

Head of Zeus Ltd
5–8 Hardwick Street
London EC1R 4RG
www.headofzeus.com

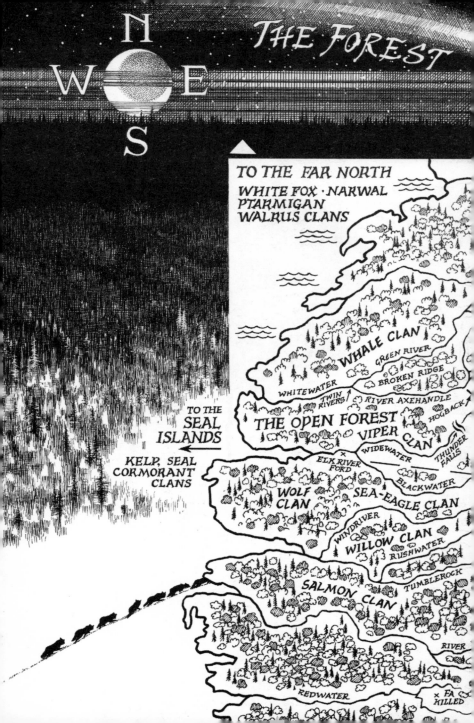

ONE

A Lynx Clan hunter saw it first. He was trudging along a ridge, checking his snares, when he spotted a brilliant spark of light moving fast across the night sky.

The hunter had seen such stars before. He knew they meant the World Spirit was shooting arrows at demons, so he was reassured as he went on his way.

Midwinter, the Dark Time, when the sun is asleep in its cave and doesn't show its face for two whole moons. No wind. Silent pines watching him pass. The only sounds the crunch of his snowshoes, the creak of his reindeer-hide parka and leggings. His breath.

As he approached the next snare he could see as clear as day, thanks to starlight and snowglow, and the rippling green radiance in the sky which the clans call the First Tree.

Good. He'd snared a willow grouse.

The horsehair noose was frozen stiff, so was the bird.

As the hunter stooped to retrieve it, something made him glance up. He was startled to see that the star had grown much brighter, and doubled in size.

On the riverbank Renn poked her head out of the shelter. 'Come on, Torak!' she called crossly. 'We need to get going!'

'I'll catch you up!' he replied without turning his head.

'No, you won't, you'll invent an excuse and stay here!'

He blew out a cloud of frosty breath. *Perfect* conditions for ice fishing. He'd hacked four beautiful holes and laid a stick across each one, from which he'd hung his lines and hooks. To attract the fish he'd made torches of folded birch bark jammed in split sticks, and set them in a row. The First Tree was helping too, shining so brightly it was sending the trout crazy, he'd already caught three. Why couldn't he stay here peacefully with the wolves?

Wolf bounded up as if he'd heard Torak's thoughts and licked the frost off his eyebrows. With a grin Torak pushed Wolf's muzzle aside. His thick winter pelt was sprinkled with snow and his breath smelt of fish. It would take too long to tell him in wolf talk that his shadow was spooking the trout, so Torak distracted him by backing away on all fours, uttering eager little grunt-whines: *Let's play!*

Lashing his tail, Wolf went down on his forelegs: *Yes, let's!* Then he pounced, soft-biting his pack-brother's arm with muffled growls and hauling him over the ice.

'You know I'm not leaving without you,' called Renn. In the glare of the torchlight she was a black figure by their shelter, but in his mind Torak saw her red hair tucked behind her ears, her pale, well-loved, infuriatingly stubborn face. 'Dark *wants* us at the Feast,' she insisted.

'Yes, but *why?*'

'I don't know, he said it's important. And he's our friend, and he never asks us for anything!'

Torak tossed a trout onto the far bank and watched Wolf race after it. He heaved a sigh.

The Moon of Long Dark was over and they were into the strange days before Sunwake, when the endless blue night was briefly lightened by a false dawn. The sky would grow pale, as if the sun was about to show itself above the Mountains – only for darkness to return as the sun retreated into its cave.

It was an edgy time when each clan did its best to ensure that in a few days the sun really would rise above the peaks. The Boar Clan burnt a whole spruce tree on a hilltop. Renn's clan, the Ravens, held the Feast of Sparks underground, while their Mage ventured even deeper to kindle the need-fire, and everyone sang and—

'Too many people,' grumbled Torak.

3

'Oh, Torak, it's not that bad, last winter you enjoyed it!'

He heard the smile in her voice and snorted a laugh. But the holes were freezing over, so he applied himself to clearing them with the butt of his ice scoop, flicking the shards for Wolf's mate, Darkfur: she loved chomping ice.

Wolf lay on the far bank, gripping the half-eaten trout in his forepaws. Behind him on the slope the cubs, Blackpaw and Tug, were pouncing on snowdrifts in futile attempts to catch lemmings. Their older brother Pebble was away guarding the pack's range. As a cub he'd been carried off by an eagle owl, and though he'd grown into a handsome young wolf, the ordeal had marked him, and he rarely relaxed.

Renn was shovelling snow onto the fire with an auroch's shoulder blade. Rip and Rek lit onto the shelter and gurgled a greeting. She gave the ravens a distracted nod. 'It's not as if we've far to go,' she told Torak. 'They're only camped a daywalk away.'

But Torak could be stubborn too. He *liked* the feel of this sleeping valley. The river dreaming under the ice, the alders asleep on its banks. Even the pines were dozing, only a single watch-tree remaining properly awake.

He'd chosen this spot because a family of beavers had dammed the river to make a pool which sheltered many fish. Not far from where he knelt, the beavers' lodge was a mound of blue snow, the air above it faintly quivering from the warmth of the furry bodies snuggled within.

Again he sighed. Renn was right. If Dark really wanted them to come...

'What's that over there?' she said in an altered voice.

He raised his head. 'Where?'

'There.'

She stood facing north, pointing at the sky.

Wolf and Darkfur had seen it too. They stood with ears pricked and tails stiff, bodies rigid with tension.

Slowly Torak rose to his feet.

It was low in the sky above the pines spiking the hilltop: a huge, brilliant, blue-white star.

'It's getting bigger,' said Renn.

In the Deep Forest the Lynx Clan hunter stood motionless, his frozen grouse forgotten at his feet. His hand crept to the fur amulet at his throat and under his breath he whispered a prayer to his clan-creature. The star had grown unbearably bright, as big as his fist.

Shielding his eyes with his arms, the hunter lurched against a pine. He heard a strange whistling noise, like a vast flock of geese rushing towards him.

The star was brighter than the sun, turning night to dazzling day. Its shadow passed across Torak, he heard a whistling like the rush of enormous wings – then a growl of thunder. 'Get under those rocks!' he yelled to Renn.

Darkfur was streaking across the ice towards her cubs, Renn shouting something he couldn't make out – then the sky was raining fire, a hot wind blowing him off his feet.

He fell with a crash. The ice was heaving, the river waking up. The thunder was louder – but how could there be thunder when there were no clouds?

A stink of singed fur, his parka was on fire. Beating out flames, he struggled to his feet.

He saw pines bending like blades of grass, others flying overhead like spears. On the far bank a blazing poplar had fallen, pinning Wolf to the ground. On the near bank the shelter had collapsed, Torak couldn't see Renn. Next moment he realized that the white thing poking through the wreckage was her hand. Who to help first, Renn or Wolf? *Who?*

A boom like a thousand thunderclaps, swelling to a deafening solid roar...

Silence.

Torak could feel the ice buckling beneath him, see the hillside shaking, trees toppling, boulders crashing – but he couldn't *hear* anything. The Forest was burning, engulfing him in fierce choking smoke.

He could no longer see Renn or Wolf.

The Lynx Clan hunter had fallen to his knees. Thunder roaring, trees thrashing, the whole sky on fire—

That was the last thing he ever saw.

The Thunderstar blasted entire valleys to cinders. It turned frozen rivers to raging torrents.

It obliterated the heart of the Forest.

TWO

Wolf growled and made to snap as Renn gently probed his flank. He slumped back, apologizing with sleeked ears and a twitch of his tail.

'Two broken ribs,' she declared. 'But he's not bringing up any blood, I think he'll be all right.'

Torak rubbed his mouth with a grimy hand.

'I'll take a look at your burns,' she said.

'What?'

'Your chest...'

He realized his parka and jerkin were torn open, his breastbone scorched raw. 'Doesn't hurt,' he muttered.

'It will soon—'

'Leave it!' he snapped.

She stared at him.

He couldn't bring himself to say sorry. Besides it was true, his chest didn't hurt. Why then did he feel this ache deep inside, as if a hook had snagged under his ribs and was tugging his innards?

Renn had been dazed when he'd dragged her from the wreck of the shelter. To shield her from flying debris he'd left her under a boulder, then rushed to rescue Wolf. Already the river had been almost impassable. Since then it had become a raging chaos of grinding ice floes and dead trees.

The earth had ceased its terrible shaking, there hadn't been a landslide for a while, but the valley still rang with the crash of falling trees. Through the bitter grey haze Torak made out the red glimmer of fires dotting the slopes. To the south the sky glowed a dreadful crimson. Above it an immense cloud of black smoke was spreading like a gigantic hand.

'I'll sew up your parka,' said Renn.

'Don't bother.'

'If I don't,' she said between her teeth, 'you will freeze.' She was grimy with soot and owl-eyed with shock, but her tone warned him to let her have her way.

She'd finished and was putting her needle back in its case when a howl rose from the far side of the river. Darkfur's long, wavering cry of grief.

Wolf lifted his head and tried to howl a reply, but broke off with a yelp. He lay down, his amber eyes dull.

Renn put her hand to her mouth. 'Not the cubs?' she whispered.

Torak nodded. 'I saw them when I found Wolf. Curled up as if they were asleep. Must've been killed by the blast.'

She was shaking her head, mouthing, *No, no, no.*

Torak remembered Tug stalking a puffball last autumn. The cub's triumphant pounce had turned to outraged yelps when the mushroom exploded, engulfing her in spores and sending her sneezing back to her mother.

'What about Pebble?' said Renn.

He didn't reply.

'Oh no … are you *sure?*'

'Work it out, Renn! If he was alive he'd have howled back by now!'

She was biting her lips. 'He was always worrying about the cubs… Maybe it's better he didn't live to—' Her voice cracked.

Torak got to his feet. 'River's rising,' he said brusquely. 'Must be blocked downstream. What gear did you salvage from the shelter?'

She opened her mouth, then shut it. 'I'm sorry. I forgot.'

'*What?* I told you to save what you could while I went to find Wolf!'

'And I didn't,' she retorted. 'And now it's been swept away by the river – like those beavers in their lodge—'

'Did you really salvage nothing?'

'I said I'm sorry!'

10

'*Sorry?* Renn, it's the middle of winter, we've no shelter, no sleeping-sack, no food—'

'And right now I don't *care!*' she flung back. 'I've no idea what just happened – or if Fin-Kedinn's alive or dead, or Dark, or the rest of my clan! Have you even *thought* about them?'

Torak rubbed his face.

Sooty water was lapping at his boots. Stooping, he lifted Wolf in his arms. 'Come on,' he muttered. 'We've got to find shelter higher up.'

Wolves are tougher than men. That was just as well, because Torak only managed a few paces carrying his pack-brother before he had to set him down.

Bees' Nest Ridge had become a near-unclimbable tangle of smoking stumps and burnt trees, their trunks studded with rocks embedded by the force of the blast.

Wolf was whining as he picked his way uphill, Renn struggling grimly over a smouldering root mass. Her face was so filthy Torak couldn't make out her clan-tattoos, the three blue-black bars on each cheek, with the red moon-bleed mark under the left one. He offered her his hand. She ignored it.

He wanted to shout: Fin-Kedinn's my foster father, I love him too! But he felt strangely cut off from her.

Darkfur's howls were still echoing across the valley.

The she-wolf had stayed on the other side of the river to grieve, and would follow when she was ready.

To Torak, Darkfur's howls and the roar of the torrent, the crash of trees, sounded weirdly muffled. There was a faint crackling in his head, and behind it a terrible lifeless silence.

He came on the twisted remains of a fawn, then the pathetic, shrivelled carcasses of woodpigeons. He felt the pain of bewildered tree spirits thronging the air. When a tree dies, its souls find the nearest seedling, which becomes their new body. But in this valley there were no saplings left alive – so where could they go?

Wolf had halted, panting and trembling. Torak caught up with him and touched foreheads, asked if he needed to rest.

Wolves don't only grunt and whine and howl, they talk with their whole bodies. Torak spoke wolf talk imperfectly, but he understood what his pack-brother was telling him. *The cubs are Not-Breath. The pack lives. We go on.*

Torak swallowed. Wolf's resilience made him feel ashamed.

Suddenly Wolf pricked his ears and turned his head. He'd heard something. A moment later Torak heard it too: the resonant caws of ravens.

Renn broke into jittery laughter. 'Rip and Rek! I'd forgotten all about them!'

The ravens' caws sounded muffled, they were calling with full beaks.

'They've found food!' cried Torak.

The reindeer had been burnt to cinders, except for one foreleg that was merely singed. Renn let Rip and Rek keep the foot, while she and Torak chiselled off every scrap of shrivelled meat, saving half and dividing the other half in three. Then they split the long bones and shared the marrow with Wolf, savouring the rich fatty goodness.

Rip and Rek strutted about, preening and shaking out their wings. They actually seemed to be *enjoying* the devastation. They loved having so many carcasses to scavenge, and the smoke was perfect for ridding their feathers of lice.

Renn was also looking steadier after some food. 'We need to rest. How about that for a shelter?' She pointed to where part of the slope had collapsed and a slab of granite lay aslant boulders. In the hollow underneath, juniper bushes were still smouldering.

Torak made a face. 'So long as another earthshake doesn't bring down that slab and squash us.'

'I'm too exhausted to care.'

The fire had swept through so fast the earth remained frozen, and without a sleeping-sack it would be vital to stay off the cold ground. Torak cleared the smoking undergrowth from the hollow and lined it with as many fire-heated stones as he could find, then he and Renn covered them with scorched boughs, making a warm base to lie on.

After that they woke a long-fire in front of the hollow, piling rocks behind to throw the heat inside. At least there was no shortage of firewood. Renn had found a blackened rowan that was still standing, it burnt well enough.

Water was a problem, as Wolf had warned them off the nearest stream: Renn guessed it had been poisoned by the smoke. The seal-gut waterskin Torak carried inside his parka for melting snow was nearly empty, and he'd forgotten to fill it at the river before they left. He and Renn took a mouthful and he gave two handfuls to Wolf.

'So what gear *do* we have?' he said, uneasily aware that they should have checked earlier.

'Only what we had on us when the – it – struck.'

Luckily they both always carried what they needed tied to their belts, so they still had their flint knives, tinder pouches, sewing kits, medicine pouches, waterskins. Torak had his slingshot, but he'd lost his axe and bow. Renn had her axe, but had lost her quiver and bow. She was particularly grieved about the arrows, black flint fletched with snow owl feathers which she'd been given the previous autumn. 'So we've got wrist-guards and finger-guards,' she complained, 'but nothing to shoot with.'

'Or any prey to shoot, by the look of it.'

'We don't know that for sure.'

Torak didn't reply.

'At least I still have my amulet.' She touched the raven foot which hung on a thong at her neck. 'And you've got yours. And I've got my duckbone whistle.'

'Mm,' he said.

He watched her take her medicine horn from her ravenskin pouch and shake earthblood into her palm. She dabbed a little on his forehead and on her own, then between Wolf's ears where he couldn't lick it off. 'Lots of demons about,' she said. 'I'll put lines of power around the shelter.'

You didn't need to be a Mage to know what she meant. Tree-roots hold demons in the Otherworld. With so many trees dead, they'd be finding it easy to escape.

Torak knew this should worry him as much as it did Renn, but something was stopping him from feeling it. The ache under his ribs was worse. And still that faint crackling in his head, like branches burning. He felt as if he was seeing Renn through a grey haze.

He realized suddenly why the silence was troubling him. No wind. Had it too been destroyed?

Renn had saved a piece of reindeer gristle and was putting it on top of the shelter as an offering to her clan guardian. Torak didn't have a clan guardian, and though he usually offered to the Forest, that felt all wrong. He felt as if he should be praying *for* the Forest.

'Pray to the First Tree,' suggested Renn.

'The First Tree. Yes.' Cutting off a lock of his long dark hair, he laid it beside her offering.

The hollow was just big enough for the three of them, although Wolf kept turning around, trying to find a position that didn't hurt. Torak was doing that too, the burns on his chest were throbbing with a vengeance. Renn

– omitting to say I told you so – smeared on spruce bark and beaver-fat salve. It stung viciously, but helped a bit.

Even without a sleeping-sack they were fairly snug, thanks to the clothes they'd got in the Far North last autumn: duckskin jerkins with the feathers against the skin, seal-hide parkas and leggings with the fur on the outside, whale-hide boots and musk-ox wool socks. Fortunately their reindeer-hide mittens were strung on sinew thongs threaded through their sleeves, so they still had these too.

Torak lay on his back with Renn's head on his shoulder. Her hair smelt of smoke. He could feel the tension in her body. 'Sorry I snapped at you earlier,' he muttered.

She shrugged. 'I should've checked the shelter.'

'Doesn't matter.'

They both knew it wasn't true.

In his mind Torak was back on the frozen river in that terrible moment when he'd had to choose between Renn and Wolf...

'Was it a star?' murmured Renn.

'I don't know.'

'But who sent it? And *why*?'

They were silent, neither wanting to voice what was in their minds. *Are we the only ones left?*

After a fitful sleep they decided to climb to the top of Bees' Nest Ridge and find out.

Through the ashen pall the sky was the colour of blood. Torak guessed it must be around the time of false dawn, but couldn't be sure.

He had tried to make Wolf stay behind in the shelter and rest, but he'd insisted on coming too – and though he was in pain, he set a faster pace than his pack-mates. At times he waited, tongue lolling, for them to catch up.

It was eerie, climbing a hillside where only the previous morning beech trees had murmured in their dreams and thrushes had squabbled over mistletoe berries, the snow beneath criss-crossed with the tracks of many creatures going about their lives.

Torak came upon more carcasses incinerated beyond recognition. Then he found something bizarre wedged between two boulders: the burnt remains of a dugout.

Only one clan made boats by hollowing oaks.

'*Boar* Clan?' panted Renn when she saw it.

Torak broke off a piece of blackened wood and turned it in his fingers.

'But the Boars are camped two daywalks to the south-east,' said Renn.

They were silent, struggling to imagine the force which could hurl a dugout all the way up this ridge.

As Torak resumed the climb, the ache under his ribs sharpened. He began to dread what he might find when he reached the top.

Wolf was waiting for him again. He was swinging his tail, his slanted amber eyes warm as they briefly met

Torak's, then glanced away. Uttering affectionate little grunt-whines, Wolf snuffle-licked his pack-brother's chin. *When the Great Bright Beast-that-Bites-Hot attacked from the Up,* Wolf told him, *you saved me.*

Torak flushed with shame. He had helped Renn first, his pack-brother second – and Wolf didn't know. He was *grateful.*

Above him tree stumps spiked the sky like broken teeth. Wolf's hindpaws wafted ash in Torak's face, making him cough. He spat into his palm. His spit was black with soot. He could taste it, gritty and acrid in his mouth. It took him a moment to realize what this meant. He was breathing in dead trees.

Below him Renn was fingering the clan-creature feathers sewn to her parka, worrying about her clan. He thought of Dark, and his hand went to the small slate wolf at his neck which his friend had carved as a gift. He called down to her: 'Crowwater Caves are deep! If they were inside when it struck, they could have survived.'

She looked at him. 'You felt the earth shake. You saw those rockfalls. What if they're trapped? What if...' She couldn't finish. Torak could find no words to comfort her.

Wolf had crested the ridge and stood with heaving flanks and drooping tail.

Torak hauled himself over the last mound of debris and stood beside his pack-brother. His knees buckled.

'What can you see?' called Renn.

He couldn't speak.

On a clear day from Bees' Nest Ridge you could see all the way north to Lake Axehead, and east to the High Mountains, south to the Deep Forest and west across the Open Forest to the Sea. Now, through the charcoal haze, all Torak could see was devastation.

He stood swaying, assailed by waves of dizzying pain, breathing in the lost souls of thousands of trees.

'Torak, what is it?' Renn was shouting.

'The Forest…' he croaked. 'It's gone.'

THREE

D ark opened his eyes.

Blackness pressing on his face. Silence so intense it made his ears ring. Shakily he put his hand in front of his nose. Couldn't see a thing. Was he dead?

Reaching out, his fingers hit rock — and everything came rushing back. He'd gone deep into the caves to wake the need-fire for the Feast while the others waited above. He'd almost arrived at the Cave of the Sun when it happened. Rocks jolting awake with a deafening roar, the tunnel twisting like an eel…

After that nothing.

He found that he was lying on his side. Bruised all over, left ankle throbbing. He flexed it. Yelped. Lay listening to his ragged breaths.

Stone dust trickled onto his face. No more shouting, Dark. Last thing you need is another rockfall.

All winter he'd been seeing omens of disaster. Faces glaring from clouds, hillsides collapsing in embers. Whatever it was, it must have happened at last.

Behind the tang of shattered stone he caught a familiar smell. Ash. A Forest fire? Was that it?

He thought of the clan gathered at the cave mouth to welcome the sun. Had they got underground in time? Was Ark with them? Or was she flying about, terrified and alone among the burning trees? What about Fin-Kedinn? Torak, Renn, Wolf?

Don't think about them. Panic now and you're lost.

Lost... He already was. No light, no sound to guide him. Just the pounding of his heart.

If only he had light! He might recognize some oddly shaped boulder, or get his bearings from the slant of a roof.

Rolling over, he clawed stone so soft it crumbled. Earthblood. Crowwater Caves were riddled with veins, not only red, but yellow and rarest purple. All had power against demons, though you had to ask the Hidden People before digging it out.

The feel of earthblood steadied Dark, and he groped for his gear. Drum smashed, Mage's belt still round his waist, pouch slung over his back. Waterskin empty: he'd been intending to fill it at the underground lake.

Wriggling out of his parka, he pulled off his fawn-skin jerkin, put his parka back on, wound the jerkin round his

21

head to protect it from the inevitable bumps. At least he wasn't cold, the caves were so deep they never froze.

The cave he was in was roomy, but standing in total darkness makes you dizzy, so he crawled, casting about blindly like a mole. Catching a whiff of colder air he veered towards it, moving slowly and carefully, as you have to underground.

He seemed to be labouring up a mound of fallen boulders. They hated being climbed, did their best to tip him off. He pictured Hidden People watching from the blackness.

The Hidden People live in rivers and rocks and they look like us, except their backs are hollow and rotten. Above all things they hate being seen. Growing up on his own in the High Mountains, Dark had learnt not to get in their way. But the Hidden People of Crowwater Caves were said to be more dangerous, and swifter to punish.

In his pouch his stone creatures clinked, and for comfort he reached inside, his fingers recognizing badger, salmon, frog. He touched something else. *The rushlights!* How could he have forgotten? He'd brought a whole bundle to light his way to the Cave of the Sun!

Most were in pieces, but he found one intact and groped for the tinder pouch at his belt.

Men twice his age would have struggled to strike a spark in pitch blackness, but Dark was a Mountain boy, and Mountain clans revere fire. It didn't take long to kindle tinder with his strike-fire and coax the rushlight awake. He screwed up his eyes against the glare, and on a boulder his giant shadow gave an edgy laugh.

Shielding the rushlight with his palm to avoid being dazzled, he saw that the cave walls were covered in handprints: red, yellow, even purple. He'd never been here before, though he'd often made such marks himself, dipping his hands in a mix of earthblood and tallow and pressing them to rocks to stop demons coming through.

But he hadn't made these handprints, they were ancient, some blurred by sooty smears where an ancestor had wiped his torch to stop it dripping. This made Dark feel a bit less alone.

It was awkward, crawling with the rushlight, so he decided to make a holder. He found a patch of the pale-grey clay the clans call moon milk, and formed some into a ball the size of a pigeon's egg. Taking a stick of kindling from his pouch, he moulded the clay ball onto one end, then stuck his rushlight upright in the clay, and gripped the other end of the stick between his teeth, like a pipe. Good. Now he had both hands free and could keep the light to one side, so it couldn't blind him.

Crawling further, he came to a special handprint. It had been made in reverse, by spitting earthblood at the ancestor's flattened hand to leave its pallid ghost outlined in purple.

Breath-painting takes time and is very powerful, because breathing leaves part of your souls in the stone. Dark felt kinship with the long-dead Mage who'd done this. Placing his hand on the print, he begged the ancestor to help him find a way out. His hand fitted exactly, except that the ancestor's little finger had been missing the last joint.

Soon afterwards Dark came to a man-high crack in the cave wall. Chill air flowed from it. 'Thank you,' he murmured, rising to his feet and edging in sideways.

Dark was thin, but he had to hold his breath to squeeze along the tunnel. It had more twists and turns than a viper, but at last he was out into another cave. More handprints. Another special one outlined in purple, very like the first.

His belly turned over. *Exactly* like the first. It fitted his hand, except it was missing the last joint of the little finger. It was the same print. He'd just gone in a circle.

His thoughts tumbled in panic. *Breathe, breathe.* What would Fin-Kedinn do now?

Shakily he swept the cave with his rushlight. Spotted a cavity in the wall at shoulder height. Hoisted himself in. Room to crawl if he kept his head low.

He hadn't gone far when his light sank to a glimmer and an icy finger touched the back of his neck.

He shut his eyes. Oh no, please, not this...

When he opened his eyes, a naked boy his own age was crouching before him.

His name had been Aki of the Boar Clan. Dark had seen him two days ago, bulky in reindeer-hide clothes as he trudged through the snow, carrying a hare carcass. Short hair in a fringe, stiff hide mantle, tusk on his chest. But then he had been alive.

The thing crouching in the tunnel had lost its name-soul, and with it all memory of who it had been. Blackened skin hung in shreds from the ghost's charcoal limbs. Its head was scorched hairless, empty eye sockets staring sightlessly at Dark.

'I'm sorry you died,' he told it. 'But you must not come closer.'

The ghost pointed at him. Its blistered lips mouthed: *Follow.* It disappeared down the tunnel.

Sometimes ghosts seek the living. Maybe Aki would lead him to survivors. Then again, sometimes ghosts wander into places from which there is no escape. And there's no telling which they'll do, as they don't know themselves. That's why you should never follow a ghost.

Dark took a breath – and followed.

The rushlight died. At the same moment he felt space opening around him. The ghost had led him to another cave. He fumbled for a second rushlight. At last it flickered awake...

He gasped. He was inside a rainbow. Everywhere he turned, crystals flashed and winked, a scintillating wonder of astonishing colour: radiant scarlet, dazzling blue, the violet glare of thunderclouds, the black glitter of eyes...

His next thought was that he shouldn't be here.

The ghost had vanished, but beyond the rushlight Dark glimpsed pale stone figures shrinking back into the gloom.

'I'm sorry!' he whispered to the Hidden People. 'I know this cave belongs to you!'

25

At the far end he spotted a low mouth of darkness, it might be a way out. 'Please, let me go in peace!'

Water dripped from shadowy stone heads emerging from the roof. As he crawled, Dark felt them turn and watch him pass.

The hole was only a forearm high and narrower than his shoulders. Taking the jerkin from round his head, he used it to bind his sprained ankle, then lay flat on his belly with the rushlight in his leading hand and eased himself in slantways.

Behind him a rock fell with a crash, echoes turning to stony laughter. *Don't come back!* warned the Hidden People.

The tunnel was so low he had to belly-crawl, pushing himself forwards on the toes of his good foot. What if it led nowhere? Was this their punishment? Don't think about that – or the weight of rock pressing down...

After an endless time he was out. Some impulse made him glance back. He'd emerged from under a giant boulder which had once fallen from the roof, and now lay on top of a rock no bigger than his head, this rock narrowing to a point on which the boulder was poised. If, while crawling, he had chanced to kick that rock loose, he would have brought down the boulder and been crushed.

Bat-squeaks reached him, high on the edge of hearing. Wings brushed his face. Relief washed over him. The bats knew him and he knew them – and he *thought* he knew this cave.

When he'd been here last its roof had been furred with sleeping bats, but now they were flitting in confusion, woken from their winter sleep by the earthshake. Dark felt a flash of pity. Once awake, they had to feed, or they were doomed. And where would they find flies in the middle of winter?

The ghost was back, squatting on a column of glistening stone, beckoning to him.

At the same moment someone slammed into Dark and pinned him against the wall. The point of a flint knife jabbed painfully under his chin. 'What *is* it?' rasped a voice in a gust of foetid breath. 'Why does it follow?'

'What? What d'you mean?'

The knife jabbed harder. 'What *is* it? What's its *name*?'

'My name's Dark, I'm—'

'*Dark*? That's not a name!'

'It's the only one I've got!'

Flinging him on his back, the man knelt over him, engulfing him in an eye-watering stink.

At least – Dark *thought* it was a man. He was old and gnarled as a storm-battered tree. The tattered remains of his parka were crusted with snot, and he'd lost most of his toes to frostbite: instead of boots he'd carelessly wrapped his stumps in lengths of gut which he'd ripped from some creature's innards without bothering to clean. His mane was a thicket of filth, and in his matted beard Dark glimpsed a half-eaten lemming and a large cave-beetle, feebly wriggling.

Belatedly Dark realized that he'd dropped his rushlight, he was seeing by the glare of a pine torch jammed in a crevice. No point trying to escape with his bad foot, he put his fists to his chest in sign of friendship. 'My name really is Dark. I'm Swan Clan but I live with the Ravens—'

'Why'd they call him *Dark* when he's white as chalk?'

'I was born without colour, that's why my clan threw me out. They hadn't yet named me, so I made one up. I thought it might help.'

The old man brought his head close to Dark's. A face as rough as bark, a mangled ruin of a nose. One eye an empty socket, the other peering suspiciously into his.

With a cackle the old man sat back on his heels, yanked a leg off a clump of putrid squirrels dangling from his waist and began to munch.

Warily Dark sat up, easing his bad foot.

The old man spat a furball at the ghost, and narrowly missed. He grinned, baring toothless black gums. Shot another searching glance at Dark. 'No wonder its clan threw it out! Hair like cobwebs, moon-milk eyes… Eyes that see ghosts.'

'I think … you can see ghosts too.'

He hawked and spat. 'And demons. The slinkers and slitherers, fighting to break through…'

Suddenly Dark knew who he was. 'Renn and Torak told me about you! People call you the Walker!'

'The Walker, the Walker,' mocked the old man through a mouthful of rotten squirrel.

28

He's mad, but not all the time, Renn had said. *Fin-Kedinn knew him long ago when he was wise, before it all went wrong.*

'Torak says you know about caves,' said Dark. 'D'you know the way out?'

Rummaging in his beard, the Walker found the beetle and crunched it up. 'The Walker used to chase demons into the Otherworld,' he mumbled. 'He knows all the deep places under the earth. But no demons here now, oh no. All gone, escaped into what's left of the world.'

Again he leant close, overpowering Dark with his stench. 'Can Chalk Boy feel it too? Everything burnt, the demons let loose?'

Dark heard a rush of wings overhead. On its column the ghost reached blackened arms towards the bats – and vanished.

Dark heard voices coming nearer. He recognized them!

'It's worse than you think,' hissed the Walker in his ear.

When Dark looked again, the old man was gone.

FOUR

'I *told* you!' shouted Sialot, a belligerent young Raven with more muscle than sense. 'We're the only ones left!'

A Viper child began to wail, which started off the others.

'We don't know that for sure,' said Dark. Inside he was appalled. The ragged group around him comprised his Ptarmigan friend Shamik, a handful of Ravens, a few Vipers who'd been at the Feast – but not Fin-Kedinn. And not Torak or Renn either, though he'd been desperately hoping that they'd joined the others while he'd been underground. 'What *happened?*' he said. 'Did anyone see?'

'They did.' An older Raven, Thull, swung his pine torch, and two men and a woman flinched from the glare.

Dark had never encountered their clan before. Their faces were red with earthblood, their heads weirdly narrow as if squashed, their front teeth filed to fangs. Dark could see these clearly as all three were grinning with fright.

'Who are you?' he said. 'What did you see?'

'They're Kelps,' Sialot said dismissively. 'But what's that got to do with—'

'Let them speak.'

The earthblood on the woman's face was cracked, her eyes blank with shock as she watched the disaster unfold in her mind. 'We were at the cave mouth,' she said dully. 'The wind was getting up, blowing snow off the trees.' Her features twisted. 'I saw a whirlwind dancing. I heard thunder from a clear sky... Terrible heat, a great star with a fiery tail. The hills quaking with fear—'

'And now we're trapped,' muttered Thull. He pinched the bridge of his nose. Among the missing were his mate and son.

Sialot opened his mouth but Dark spoke first. 'Maybe not. I'll lead until we find Fin-Kedinn – and I'll tell you why I don't think we're trapped. I've been smelling ash, and if ash can get in, that means we can get out.'

Sialot scowled, wishing he'd thought of that. The others waited for Dark to go on.

'Anyone hurt?' he said. 'Anyone got water?' No to both. Taking Thull's torch, he indicated a shadowy tunnel. 'Lake's not far, we can—'

'No, we can't!' cut in Sialot. 'There's something terrible down there.'

'What do you mean?' said Dark.

'Giant bear, from the sound of it,' said a Viper woman.

'Or a demon,' said Thull. 'We all heard it, it won't let us near the water.'

'I was going to tell you,' said Sialot with a curl of his lip. 'But you were so keen to take charge.'

'Well, now you've told me,' snapped Dark. 'Everyone stay here, I'll be back.'

Can't be a bear, he thought as he headed down the tunnel with the torch. No bear would den this deep. More likely one of the Hidden Peoples' tricks.

He caught the drip-drip of water and the tunnel opened out. Beyond the torchlight, impenetrable black: he sensed the lake only by its chill. He took a step forwards.

Echoing growls warned him back.

Certainly sounded huge, the growls reverberating through the rocks beneath his feet. He told himself that caves often do odd things to noises.

Or could he be wrong about that bear?

The growls sank to menacing rumbles. Dark spotted a fissure near the water. The noise was coming from inside.

He crouched before it.

A savage snarl.

Torch shaking in his fist, Dark peered in.

A monstrous shadow, a gleam of eyes…

Dark blinked. *'Pebble?'*

Subdued voices drifted across the lake. The search parties led by Sialot and Thull were holding torches to every crevice, watching the smoke: if there was a way to the world above, the smoke would tell them. As yet, nothing.

Nearby, the Vipers were doing the same with the third torch. The Kelps – whom the others had shunned because they were strangers – were working in darkness, feeling the rocks by hand. Dark was using a broken rushlight, while talking softly to Pebble in the hopes of enticing the young wolf out of his hiding-place.

Dark could hear him prowling inside, but the fissure that led to Pebble's cave was so low he would have had to crawl to get in – and Pebble, panting and yawning with fright, was in no state to be approached, not even by someone he trusted. His fur had been singed to the skin and his pads scorched, Dark heard him yelp at every step. Who knew what horrors he'd endured?

From his pouch Dark took a small slate otter and placed it within the crack. As a cub Pebble had loved licking stones, it was how he'd got his name. Maybe Dark's smell on the otter would give comfort, even lure him out.

'It's all right, Pebble,' Dark whispered, kneeling at the fissure. From within came the near-inaudible keen of a wolf in pain.

Dark reached in his arm and waited, his mind seething with terrible images. Why was Pebble on his own? What had happened to Darkfur and the cubs, and Wolf and Torak and Renn?

Breath warmed his palm. In the gloom he glimpsed a raw red nose. 'Pebble, it's me...'

A cry rang across the lake: 'We've got something!'

Running footsteps. Pebble retreated into his cave.

'Come and see!' panted Thull.

Chill air was flowing from a crack at the top of a huge mound of boulders. People were feverishly heaving them aside. Shamik, who had a withered arm, was holding the last remaining torch.

Dark scrambled up and started helping. It was backbreaking work and he could feel everyone wondering, what if this only leads to another cave? What if we're trapped?

Suddenly icy wind blew back his hair. Torchlight flared, and a man's grimy hand reached through from the other side.

'Dark, is that you?' cried Fin-Kedinn.

'And that was when you found us,' finished Dark.

'You did well,' said Fin-Kedinn.

Dark flushed. The Raven Leader rarely praised, and only when he meant it.

With people working from both ends it hadn't taken long to clear the way out, but the first wild reunions had swiftly turned to horror. Choked-back sobs for loved ones still missing, gasps at the devastated valley, cruelly visible in the false dawn.

Fin-Kedinn hadn't given them time to brood. He'd sent some to seek firewood and survivors. The rest were building shelters near the cave mouth.

Pebble was still refusing to leave his hiding-place. Dark had left a scent trail with scraps cut from his parka, hoping that in time it would encourage the young wolf to follow.

'I didn't tell them about the Walker,' Dark said in an undertone. 'D'you want me to go back in and find him?'

Fin-Kedinn shook his head. 'He'll come out when he's ready.'

They were at the edge of camp, the Raven Leader seated on a boulder with his one-eared dog Grip at his feet, Dark squatting with Ark perched on his shoulder. Usually dazzling white, the raven was grey with soot, furiously preening. Dark too was grey all over, ash gritty in his mouth.

Fin-Kedinn was sorting a pile of half-charred branches into kindling, torches and firewood. 'Tell me again what he said.'

'He said it's worse than we think.'

The Raven Leader frowned. 'Your foot. Is it broken?'

'I'm fine, it's just sprained.'

Fin-Kedinn looked at him, his blue eyes startling in his blackened face. 'How many can you see?' he said quietly.

Dark's throat worked. Being able to see ghosts had never troubled him before – but now… 'So many. Willows, Rowans, Vipers, Boars … Thull's mate and son. I'll have to tell him.'

'Not yet.' Fin-Kedinn held out his strike-fire. 'You're better at this, take over.'

It wasn't long before Dark had lit two torches. He handed back the strike-fire, aware that Fin-Kedinn had given him the task as a distraction. Where were Torak and Renn? Dark dreaded catching sight of them among the ghosts thronging the edge of camp.

A distant howl floated on the wind. Another wolf answered. Both desolate with grief.

Dark caught his breath. Beneath the grime the blood drained from Fin-Kedinn's face.

'That's Wolf and his mate,' said Dark. 'They're mourning the dead.'

Wolf's flank still hurt when he sneezed, and he was sneezing a lot, because of all the ash.

Wrinkling his muzzle, he watched Tall Tailless smash the Bright Hard Cold with a rock, the pack-sister kneel to fill her deerskin with Wet. Wolf took one sniff and leapt, knocking the skin from her paws. He whined an apology but couldn't make her understand that the Wet was bad – so he told Tall Tailless, who told her in tailless talk.

36

They looked dejected as they struggled on. Just as well they couldn't see the Breaths-that-Walked on the ruined hillside. All the lost spirits. Taillesses, prey, trees...

But Wolf had no time for pity, he was worried about the pack. When the Great Bright Beast had attacked from the Up it hadn't only eaten the Forest, it had killed his cubs and ravaged his mate with grief. Wolf *missed* her. That hurt far worse than his injured flank.

He was also worried about Tall Tailless, who was wounded inside and hiding it. Wolf felt cut off from his pack-brother by a strange prickly blackness.

The pack-sister had made a Den below the top of the hill and they were settling to sleep. Wolf prowled the slopes, keeping watch against demons. This was hard, as the stink of dead Forest had eaten all the smells.

The ravens who belonged to the pack cawed a warning: they'd spotted a demon sneaking towards the Den. With a growl Wolf chased it away.

When he returned, only the pack-sister was huddled asleep. To his horror Wolf saw Tall Tailless standing on the hilltop, at the very edge. He was swaying, and though his eyes were open, Wolf knew he was asleep.

Hurtling uphill, Wolf flung himself at his pack-brother and knocked him backwards onto the ground. He stood over him, barking.

Tall Tailless blinked and rubbed his face. He stared at the Up. High overhead, the Bright White Eye was half-shut, her many little cubs glinting around her.

Tall Tailless asked Wolf if he could hear the Tree of Light. Wolf said no, it was gone. His pack-brother heaved a sigh that hurt so much Wolf felt it too. He tried to lick Tall Tailless's muzzle but he pushed him away. Wolf didn't know what was wrong, or how to make him better.

The Dark was growing lighter when Tall Tailless got to his feet and stumbled off to join his mate.

The ravens were playing in the Up, flying beak-to-tail. Another raven joined them, this one grey instead of black. In a snap Wolf realized what this meant. Eagerly he raced after the birds.

Yes! Down in that smoky valley, the glimmer of small Bright Beasts-that-Bite-Hot! *Clever* birds, they'd found the tailless pack that smelt of ravens!

It didn't take long to fetch Tall Tailless and the pack-sister. When she spotted the Den of the taillesses she began to whimper. Now she was running, scrambling over whatever lay in her path – and the leader of the raven pack was limping towards her, leaning on his stick, and she was throwing herself at him and he was holding her tight.

Wolf was glad. *Now* he could go and fetch his mate. Soon the pack would be together again.

And then, surely, Tall Tailless would get better.

FIVE

Renn, picking her way by torchlight to the underground lake, saw Darkfur emerge from Pebble's hiding-place. The black she-wolf was barely visible as she padded to the water to drink, Pebble creeping behind her, whining at every step.

It was the first time the young wolf had left his cave, and Renn froze. Dark, kneeling by the lake, was speaking softly to encourage him.

Renn felt a sneeze begin. She pinched her nose. No use. The sneeze echoed. Pebble lost his nerve and shot back into his cave.

'Sorry,' called Renn.

Dark clenched his fists and stared fixedly at the lake. She was surprised. Dark never got angry.

'We need you in camp,' she told him with an edge to her voice.

'Coming,' he replied without turning round. From his parka he drew a young hedgehog with singed bristles and set it down to drink. He was rubbing his forehead, as if the clan-tattoos he'd got last autumn were bothering him. Renn thought he looked like a thin, exhausted ghost.

Well, I'm exhausted too, she thought irritably.

Five days since she and Torak had reached camp, and she'd barely slept. A trickle of survivors had swelled numbers to over sixty: many burnt or injured by flying debris, some so shocked they could do nothing but shake. And always people wondered why more didn't come. In winter the Mountain clans followed the reindeer into the Forest, and the Sea clans retreated inland from the gales that battered the coast. All had been seeking shelter under the trees when the Thunderstar struck.

By common consent, Fin-Kedinn had been chosen as camp Leader. He'd been tireless: settling fights, organizing supplies, encouraging by his presence. When he'd called a clan meet, even the word had heartened people. Clan meets were what they'd had before the Thunderstar.

'More survivors just came in,' said Renn.

'I know.'

'Dark, I need your help—'

'I said I'm coming!'

They glared at each other.

I'm hating this too! she wanted to shout. I'm worried Fin-Kedinn's working too hard, and I haven't seen Torak for days, and I can't stop wondering, what if the whole Forest's gone?

Even thinking that made her breathless and sick. The Forest was everything. It gave shelter and fire, bark for rope-making and nets, nuts and berries for medicine and food. Hunters and prey depended on it to survive, and it never let them down. How could it be gone?

'Someone's coming,' said Dark.

'Oh no,' muttered Renn.

The Kelp woman was making her way towards them holding a slimy, fishy-smelling mess.

'Go away,' said Renn and Dark together.

'Herring skins for the wolf's paws,' Halut said flatly. 'Very good for burns.'

'We know that, we're Mages,' snapped Renn. 'Why have you been hoarding herrings instead of handing them in for rations?'

'Only the skins, we keep dried ones for medicine. I've soaked them. Is the wolf in there?'

'He won't let you near,' said Dark. 'He hates strangers.'

'Then you do it.' Halut dumped the fish skins in Renn's hands and turned to go. She hesitated. 'Do wolves really have golden eyes?'

Renn was startled. 'Surely you've seen a wolf?'

'There aren't any on our island.' The narrow face caked in earthblood looked wistful. Then she scowled. 'You shouldn't call him Pebble. Wolves are sacred.' She touched her fang-like teeth. 'That's why we do this.'

'Well, that's his name,' retorted Renn. But after Halut had gone she felt bad. No wonder the Kelps were prickly. Everyone was ganging up on them. 'It's just they look so weird,' she said.

Dark snorted. 'I look weird too.'

She didn't reply. She'd realized why he was down here, avoiding the latest survivors. Their clan-tattoos were thirteen red dots on the forehead. Same as his. 'Swans,' she murmured. 'Oh, Dark, I'm sorry.'

He shrugged. 'Doesn't matter.'

Yes, it does, she thought.

When Dark was a boy, his father had taken him into the mountains and abandoned him. For seven winters he'd survived on his own. Renn couldn't imagine how it must feel to come face to face with the clan which had left you to die.

'D'you think the herring skins will work?' he said in a voice that warned her he didn't want to talk about it.

'Um – no. But it'll give the wolves something to do.'

Ever since the Thunderstar, Pebble had been desperate to be a cub again, staying safe in his cave. His mother, having howled herself hoarse for her dead cubs, had found fresh purpose in caring for him. She'd become adept at dodging the camp dogs, and brought him any scraps she could scavenge from the surrounding hills.

She was with Pebble now, and the tiny cave was

cramped. Renn squeezed inside while Dark knelt in the entrance, holding the torch. Renn bound Pebble's paws with strips of fish skin, both wolves watching every move. When she'd finished, she couldn't help smiling. Pebble was already nibbling the binding on one forepaw, his mother licking his hindpaws.

'Shows how much Halut knows about wolves,' Renn said, giving Darkfur's flank an affectionate scratch. The she-wolf swept the floor with her tail. 'Still, I suppose it might help—' She broke off.

'What is it?' said Dark.

'Back up, will you, I'm coming out. Found something snagged in her underfur.'

A boy was calling from the cave mouth: 'Scouts have returned, clan meet's about to start!'

Renn and Dark ignored him. They were staring at what lay in her palm.

A spruce twig: its needles a fresh, vibrant green.

Renn waylaid Fin-Kedinn in the Ravens' shelter as he was leaving for the clan meet. He turned the spruce twig in his fingers, then handed it back. 'Tell no one,' he said under his breath.

She gaped at him. 'But surely—'

'It may not mean what you think. It could've caught in her fur before the Thunderstar struck.'

43

'*Or* it means there are *living trees* out there! It'd give people hope!'

'Hope which might be dashed, Renn. We tell no one till we're sure.'

'But—'

'Enough! Time to start the clan meet.' His face was carved sandstone, his voice brooked no argument. Smouldering, Renn obeyed.

The whole camp was gathered around the long-fire. It was an overcast night, the sky heavy with snow. Firelight flickered on sooty faces streaked with mourning marks.

Among the scouts, Renn spotted Torak. He was gaunt with exhaustion, frowning at the sky. She failed to catch his eye.

Dark was edging through the crowd towards her when one of the newcomers spotted him. A tall man with an angular face, he took in Dark's appearance and his jaw dropped. He recovered swiftly, forcing a smile and reaching to touch the younger man's shoulder. To Renn's astonishment, Dark flung him off with a snarl, leaving the man aghast.

The man's long hair was nutbrown, but in his hollow cheeks and prominent jaw Renn detected a resemblance to Dark. As her friend approached she said quietly, 'That man, is he—'

'My father,' Dark said between his teeth. Next moment he was asking the clan guardians to watch over the camp in a clear voice which betrayed no sign of what he was feeling.

Fin-Kedinn declared the clan meet open and people quietened down, eager to hear from the scouts. As the speaking-stick was passed from hand to hand, a shocked silence fell.

'No trace of the Boar Clan...'

'Or the Otters. The cliffs on the eastern shore of Lake Axehead have collapsed, nothing left of their camp...'

'Rowan Clan hunters say the Thunderstar struck the Mountains, shattered a whole peak...'

'I heard that it destroyed the cave where the sun sleeps! The sun is dead!'

'They say where it struck it made a boiling lake. This cooled to a swamp, and from it crawled creatures that have no souls. People call them Skin-Takers... They prey on the dead and the dying.'

'Crowwater valley's flooded for two daywalks downstream.' This from Torak. 'Landslip prevented me finding out why.'

'I know why.'

It wasn't a scout who'd spoken but a Salmon Clan hunter who'd just arrived with his daughter. A silent child about eight summers old, she was clutching her father's wrist, which ended in a stump, an old injury long since healed.

Fin-Kedinn nodded at Torak to pass the man the speaking-stick.

'My name's Gaup,' he told the throng. 'Crowwater's blocked because it flows into the Widewater. That's blocked too. Half the Hogback's collapsed, it's buried the river upstream of Thunder Falls.'

Jaws hung open, heads shook in disbelief. The Widewater was the greatest river in the Forest – and the richest in salmon. If it wasn't flowing by spring, the salmon would not swim up from the Sea. And the clans depended on the salmon run. It had never been known to fail.

Sialot sprang to his feet. 'Why worry about spring? What about *now*? How can we hunt when there isn't any prey? How can we fish when the rivers are poisoned? And why,' he added accusingly, 'are we feeding strangers when we haven't enough for ourselves?'

Roars of agreement, and menacing glances at Gaup.

'I don't *mind* if they're able-bodied,' Sialot went on. 'But we can't waste supplies on strangers who can't pull their weight!'

Neither Gaup nor his daughter responded to his slurs, but Shamik clutched her withered arm to her chest. Dark put his arm around her and glared at Sialot.

'What you're all ignoring,' shrilled a Willow woman, 'is that this is *our fault*! We angered the World Spirit, that's why it sent the Thunderstar!'

'It's not *our* fault, it's the Kelps!' yelled a Viper man. 'Everyone knows Sea clans hate the Forest!'

'And Forest clans dishonour the Sea!' Halut shot back. 'This is your fault, not ours!'

'What about the Mages?' shouted a Whale girl. 'Why didn't they see this coming?'

Until now Fin-Kedinn had stood watching the angry, frightened people. Taking the speaking-stick from Gaup, he waited.

A hush fell.

'You chose me to lead,' Fin-Kedinn said calmly. 'So that's what I'll do. All this talk about differences – but one thing binds us *together*. Whether you're from the Sea, the Forest, the Mountains or the Ice – each of us is a hunter. Like all hunters, when we kill prey, we keep the Pact which our ancestors made with the World Spirit: we waste nothing. Like all hunters we've known bad times – the sickness, the demon bear. We've come together and survived. That's what we'll do now.'

Muttering and head-shaking. Not many were persuaded.

'It's *not true* the sun is dead,' continued the Raven Leader. 'The false dawn grows longer every day, you *know* this! You know it means that soon we'll see the sun. It's *not true* that every river is poisoned! The underground lake isn't, and yesterday Thull found sweet water to the south-west. It's *not true* that all prey is dead! The Swans tell me they've seen fresh reindeer tracks. If one reindeer survived – and wolves and ravens too – other creatures may be alive. And who knows – ' he glanced at Renn – 'there may be valleys where the Forest still lives. We will find them.'

He paused to let that sink in. 'Tomorrow we go ice fishing and we track that reindeer. Tonight we finish what we started before the Thunderstar: we hold the Feast of Sparks to wake the sun.'

Renn and Dark had performed the Sun Chant and while everyone was settling to eat, she showed Torak the spruce twig. He wasn't as encouraged as she'd expected, but he went down into the caves to ask Darkfur where she'd been.

He returned soon after, shaking his head. 'Many lopes, that's all she said. Wolves don't know about north and south.'

'I still think it's a good sign,' said Renn.

He sat cross-legged, passing a scrap of green amber from palm to palm. Renn asked where he'd got it. From one of the Kelps, he said.

Nearby, a squabble broke out. 'Oh, what now?' muttered Renn.

Camp rations were a bitter gruel of scorched pine-nuts, acorns and tough auroch's ear mushrooms, but for the Feast this had been enriched with whatever supplies the clans had been able to salvage after the Thunderstar. The Ravens had contributed some dried salmon flatcakes, the Willows a few pickled beaver feet, the Sea-eagles smoked cods' tongues. The Swans had given dried elk livers, the Kelps a pouch of herring roe in seal oil. The fight was over whether it was wrong to mix Forest food with that from the Sea.

Wearily Fin-Kedinn rose and raised the speaking-stick. 'Some of you,' he said into the resulting silence, 'have forgotten the story our elders used to tell. Listen – and remember.'

It began to snow, fluffy flakes falling gently on tired faces.

'In the time that was, when even the stars were dark,' said Fin-Kedinn, 'the First Tree began to grow. Its branches pushed up the sky. Its roots made the earth. From its seeds grew the Forest.' His voice was a beam of light in the darkness, leading away from the horror of the present to the murmurous green past.

'The World Spirit took a handful of leaves and blew on them: they became hunters and prey, and for a time all was well.' He paused. 'Then the Great Wave attacked the land. As the floodwaters rose, all creatures feared they would drown. So they banded together to make a raft. Beavers felled trees. Our ancestors twisted ropes out of horses' tails. Aurochs and boars hauled logs, our ancestors tied them together. Frogs and mice mixed mud with the underfur of deers and wolves, and plugged gaps. Birds plucked their down to keep the people warm. Salmon laid their eggs on kelp fronds, so that everyone had food while they were afloat. And when at last the waters sank, hunters and prey returned to the Forest and were saved.'

Watching the whole camp hanging on her uncle's words, Renn's heart swelled with love for him. Fin-Kedinn had cared for her since she was little, when her father was killed. Now he was caring for them all.

It was snowing more thickly, cloaking the filthy camp in glistening white.

According to the ice clans, a snowfall means the moon is making a new face for itself of walrus ivory, and sweeping the shavings from its shelter. Renn couldn't see the moon, but she knew it was there. It hadn't forsaken them. There was still hope.

She turned to Torak. He too was watching the sky, but his face was drawn. 'You're not eating,' she said softly.

'I'm not hungry. When did you last see the First Tree?'

'What...? But it's snowing, we won't see it now.'

He frowned down at the green amber in his hand.

'Torak, what's wrong? What aren't you telling me?'

He looked at her. She saw his clan-tattoos, two dotted lines on his cheekbones with the scar cutting across the left. She saw the quartered circle tattooed on his forehead. She saw his vivid, bloodshot, light-grey eyes. She gasped. The little green flecks that she loved... They were gone.

'What's happened to you?' she whispered.

'Come with me.' Taking her wrist, he pulled her to her feet. 'Someone you need to see.'

SIX

'Oh, it's gone all right,' mumbled the Walker through a mouthful of rotten squirrel. 'Wolf boy already knows. No more First Tree, Thunderstar blew it away.'

Squatting on his haunches, he snatched a pebble, scrutinized it, chucked it in the underground lake.

Renn watched the ripples spreading till they lapped her boots. He was the same filthy, mad old man she'd encountered in the past: half-naked yet oblivious to the cold, ropes of yellow-green snot dangling from what remained of his nose. Why were they listening to what he said? It couldn't be true.

But deep inside, she knew that it was.

The First Tree *gone*? How was that possible? The First

Tree lit the way in the Dark Time. It kept the Forest alive.

Dark was shaking his head in disbelief, Torak pacing, fingering the piece of green amber. Wolf and Darkfur had gone scavenging in the hills, and from the world above came faint sounds of the Feast.

Fin-Kedinn, seated on a boulder, said quietly: 'How can you be sure of this, old friend?'

Through his thicket of hair the Walker's eye gleamed. 'The clans call this place the Crowwater Caves, but their old name means Roots of the First Tree. All gone now, oh, yes. Nothing to keep the demons inside.'

From the tattered remains of his leggings he drew an icicle and set it on the ground. 'White for snow,' he muttered. 'And for bone, where souls live and die...'

'But the First Tree *can't* be gone!' Renn burst out. 'Look at this!' She thrust the spruce twig in his face.

'So what?' Snatching the twig, he threw it in the lake. 'If the First Tree doesn't return, what's left of the Forest will die, then everything else dies too.'

'And you don't care,' growled Torak.

The old man cackled. Tragedy had blighted him long ago, nothing could reach him now.

Fin-Kedinn made to speak, but at that moment Pebble shot from his cave and hurtled towards the Walker. To everyone's astonishment the young wolf was whimpering with delight, lashing his tail, flailing his forepaws, covering the old man in ecstatic snuffle-licks.

Grinning, the Walker took Pebble's muzzle in his hand and peered at him. 'I know you,' he murmured. 'Little lost cub in the mountains, stuck in the snow!'

Rising on his hind legs, Pebble put his forepaws on the old man's shoulders and started licking his face. With a laugh the Walker pushed him off. Before Renn knew what he was up to, he'd snatched her tinder pouch from her belt.

'Give that back!' she yelled.

'Just *borrowed*,' he taunted, holding it out of reach.

'Let him have it, Renn,' Fin-Kedinn told her. 'He'll give it back in time.'

Mumbling to himself, the Walker drew her blue slate strike-fire from the pouch and laid it beside the icicle. Pebble settled down to lick his toeless stumps.

'Blue for the Sea,' muttered the Walker. 'That's for secrets, and seeing near and far. Now what's for red? Ah!' With one horny thumbnail he gashed his forearm, smeared blood on a stone, placed it beside the strike-fire and the icicle. Pebble made to lick them. The Walker batted him away. 'Red for fire, and love and hate.'

'Where's all this getting us?' said Dark.

'And what about the First Tree?' demanded Torak. 'You told me you'd *help*! Instead you're playing games!'

Fin-Kedinn cast him a warning look. To the Walker: 'You said, "*if* it doesn't return". Does that mean there's a chance we can bring it back?'

'Clever Fin-Kedinn,' chuckled the old man, studying the icicle and the stones. 'Never misses a thing.'

'So how do we do it?' said Fin-Kedinn.

'Chalk Boy knows, and Raven girl. The Walker remembers her from five summers ago. Oh, how she loved her bow! Spat fury when he threatened to hurt it...'

Renn furrowed her brow. Why mention her bow? 'Some kind of ... Rite?'

Putting out his mossy tongue, he licked his slimy nose. 'It must be done in the dark of the moon. *This* moon!'

'That doesn't leave us much time,' said Renn.

The Walker barked a laugh. 'Then you'd better hurry! Otherwise the Moon of Green Snow won't be very green, not without the First Tree!'

'The Moon of Green Snow,' said Dark. 'That's the moon after next—'

The Walker gaped at him, feigning admiration. '*Clever* Chalk Boy!' he sneered. 'Takes a *real* Mage to know the order of the moons!'

Dark ignored that. He was staring at the blue slate and the reddened pebble as if they held a clue. 'The Moon of Green Snow – that's when we help the World Spirit defeat the Great Auroch by shooting arrows at the sky...'

Renn snapped her fingers. '*That's* what these are for, arrows!'

'Arrow*heads*,' corrected the Walker.

'So – we make special ones of different-coloured stones?' queried Dark.

'None of them stolen, or it won't work.' The old man blew his nose in his hand, smeared it on his beard.

Renn and Dark were nodding excitedly. Dark pointed at the strike-fire. 'Blue for the Sea.'

'Red for fire.' Renn indicated the bloodied pebble. Then the icicle. 'White for snow,' they said together.

The Walker bared his toothless black gums. 'They can't be ordinary stones, oh, no. Not flint, or slate, or quartz. Have to be bluest of blue and reddest of red, clearest of clear...'

Dark looked at him. 'If we find them, what do we do then?'

'A summoning?' Renn said doubtfully.

The Walker fixed her with his eye, and she caught a glimmer of sanity, like an agate at the bottom of a pool. 'An ancient Rite. No one remembers it but the Walker.' His voice became deep and resonant: the voice of the Otter Clan Mage he used to be. 'Four arrows to bring back the First Tree. A bridge of light to fly beyond moon and stars... The Voice of Then becomes the Song of Now... If the brightest souls in the Forest can sing the arrows on their way, they will bring back the First Tree – and the world will be saved.'

He hawked and spat, vigorously scratched his scalp.

'You said *four* arrows,' put in Renn.

Faster than thought, the Walker snatched Torak's green amber. 'Give it back!' yelled Torak.

'Torak, be still!' ordered Fin-Kedinn.

'Green for the Forest that gives life to hunters and prey,' intoned the old man. He made a face at the amber,

55

tossed it to Torak. 'Right colour, wrong stone. Has to be *heart*stone, that's the most vital of all. Has to be, or the Rite won't work.'

Renn was scowling. 'What's heartstone?'

'Never heard of it!' cried Dark.

'Is Chalk Boy *stupid*?' roared the Walker, sending Pebble hurtling back to his cave. 'Heartstone is *greenest of green*! In the deepest deeps of the Deep Forest they will find it!'

'And where's that?' snapped Renn.

Again that fugitive glint of sanity. 'Some places in the Forest you can only find when you're lost.'

She flung up her arms. 'Not another riddle!'

'He means the sacred grove,' said Torak in an altered voice. They stared at him. The Walker was nodding.

'How do you know?' Fin-Kedinn said softly.

'I feel it here.' Torak touched below his chest. 'A pain. Something hooked under my ribs, pulling me towards it.'

'I don't understand,' said Dark. 'What is—'

'The sacred grove,' Renn explained, 'is many daywalks away in the Deep Forest. Torak was born there.' She turned to the Walker. 'Even if we can find the heartstone and make all four arrows, you haven't told us how to do the Rite.'

'You haven't told us,' mocked the Walker in a whiny, little-girl voice.

He made to leave, but Fin-Kedinn caught his arm. 'Help us do this, old friend! You were a Mage once—'

'Not any more!' snarled the Walker, shaking him off.

'Chalk Boy knows about stones, Raven girl can shoot, leave it to them!'

He shambled into the gloom – but next moment he was back, pinning Renn against a boulder. 'Watch the wolf boy,' he breathed. 'Darkness in his souls, the black web rising… He got too close to the trees, now he can't get out.'

'Torak, you'll seek the heartstone in the Deep Forest,' Fin-Kedinn told him. 'It'll take a day or so to gather your gear and I want it done in *secret*, no one must know that you're leaving or where you're heading.'

'Why?' said Renn and Torak together.

The Raven Leader lifted his broad shoulders. 'You have your Mage's sense, Renn, and I have a Leader's sense for when people are lying. There are those in camp I don't trust. It's just a feeling, but I don't want trouble following Torak. Best we keep this secret. Yes?'

'I'm going with him,' said Renn.

'She's safer here,' Torak said to Fin-Kedinn.

'No one's safe!' she shot back. 'And it's my choice, not yours.'

'You'd help Dark and me if you stayed in camp,' said her uncle.

'I'll help Torak more. Besides, Wolf or the ravens might find prey, and that might lead us to wherever that twig came from, where the trees are still alive.'

The Raven Leader rubbed his beard. To her surprise he laughed. 'Renn, you make it sound almost straightforward.' He turned to Dark. 'But you *will* stay here. I need you, so do the injured.'

'No, *please!*' begged Dark. 'The Walker's right, I know about stones, I can help Torak and Renn find them! *And* I'm good at stone-working, I can make the arrowheads—'

'You won't get far on a sprained ankle,' the Raven Leader reminded him.

Dark had no answer to that. He stood glowering, a muscle working in his jaw. Renn felt intensely sorry for him. She knew he was desperate to escape the Swans.

'So apart from finding the four stones,' Torak said drily, 'including this heartstone nobody's heard of, all we have to do is work out what the old man meant by the Voice of Then and the Song of Now, *and* find the brightest souls in the Forest.'

Fin-Kedinn looked at him, then at Renn. 'What the Walker said has meaning, even if we don't yet understand. Remember everything he told you. Every word may count. And be warned. Demons won't be the worst things you encounter out there. At the best of times Deep Forest clans don't welcome strangers. If they've survived, who knows what they'll do?' He paused. 'When disaster strikes and people are frightened, they turn on each other. It's *people* you'll have to fear the most.'

SEVEN

Torak is frightened. He's trapped in a crackling tangle of charred branches. Cold rasping his lungs, cheeks stiff with frozen tears. Where is he? What is this black web? Why can't he break free?

With an immense effort he flexes his fingers inside his mittens. He rolls onto all fours.

Ice beneath him. Around him dense freezing fog. 'Smoke-frost,' he murmurs. The breath of the World Spirit, who walks in winter as a woman with red willow-branch hair.

The black web is still with him, but now it's inside his head. Through the drifting whiteness he glimpses the desolation of the Dead Lands. He remembers. He and Renn are heading for the Deep Forest.

Lurching to his feet, he staggers with hands outstretched like a blind man.

A giant shadow looms from the fog.

The bear is as startled as Torak, standing on its hind legs, too close to avoid. With an explosive grunt it veers past him, its forepaw catching his cheek, knocking him over.

Shaken, he sits up. Slips his hand out of his mitten, touches his face. The heel of the bear's pad merely brushed his cheek, but it has scraped the skin like granite. He blinks at the blood on his fingers. The fact that he can feel pain is reassuring. It tells him he's alive. Inside him the black web has dwindled to a shadow.

A great grey wolf is racing towards him, uttering anxious little grunt-whines. For a heartbeat Torak doesn't know who he is. Then he's sinking both hands in Wolf's thick winter pelt, inhaling his beloved sweet-grass scent and meaty breath. *This is Wolf, I am his pack-brother. Hold onto Wolf.*

Someone was coming. 'Didn't you hear me shouting?' cried Renn. She was panting, hood flung back, red hair curling with fog. 'Oh, Torak, you were sleepwalking again!'

He stretched his mouth in a grin. 'Sorry. I… didn't expect to meet a bear in the middle of winter.'

She was biting her lips to stop them trembling. 'Thunderstar must've woken it, like those bats in the caves. Who knows how many more bears will have come out of their dens?'

The fog lifted as they made their way back to their shelter. Two days till Sunwake. In the east the false dawn was radiant gold, but in the west it was still night, the half-eaten moon hanging bright in slatey darkness.

For three days they'd been struggling through the Dead Lands towards the Jaws of the Deep Forest. With landmarks gone and whole valleys laid waste, they'd reckoned by the stars, picking their way through charcoal ruins haunted by demons and the lost spirits of trees. If they could find the Jaws, they planned to head south, over the great ridge the clans called the Shield – then follow the Windriver upstream to the sacred grove.

Renn touched his shoulder. 'Are spirits troubling you in your sleep? Is that what's wrong? I can do a charm—'

'No, Renn. No.'

'Then what? Tell me!'

His throat had closed. He turned away so that he wouldn't see the hurt in her face. He couldn't bear it. He felt so ashamed. He was her mate. He was no good to her like this.

It was the same with Wolf, who kept bringing him gifts to cheer him up: a branch, or a frozen lemming. It broke Torak's heart that he couldn't respond.

The narrow valley where they'd camped was eerily quiet. The trees here had been toppled, though not burnt by the Thunderstar. Stripped of branches and bark, every flayed trunk lay pointing the same way.

Torak could feel their spirits in the air. He sensed the black web waiting. It came and went without warning.

Darkness in his souls, the black web rising… He got too close to the trees… How had the Walker known?

Three winters ago Torak had spirit walked in a yew. That never-to-be-forgotten experience had taught him that trees are different from all other creatures, their souls not separate, but *linked*. It had also nearly killed him. His spirit had been swept away, a tiny spark in a vastness of green, from yew to sapling to towering oak, faster than wolf could run or raven fly…

Was that what was happening? Was he caught in the torment of the devastated Forest?

Renn was speaking his name. 'Torak, *please!* Talk to me!'

His throat worked. 'Let's get going,' he muttered. 'It's better when I'm on the move.'

Later, when she wasn't looking, he raked his fingernails deliberately down his cheek. The pain felt good. It kept the black web at bay.

Maybe that's the answer, he thought. More danger, more pain. Yes. Like sealing a wound with fire.

The red clay mask glared at them from the boulder. A bristling mane of thorns, a vicious slash of a mouth, eyes and teeth of splintered ice. *Go back!* it shrieked with silent rage. *This is the Deep Forest. You do not belong.*

It had been summer when they'd been here last, paddling the River Blackwater between the Jaws of the

Deep Forest: two towering rocks leaning crazily over the water. Now the Jaws lay in ruins, toppled by the Thunderstar. What Renn remembered as a shadowy green valley of watchful, moss-hung trees was a desolation of broken stumps. To the south loomed the forbidding grey rockface of the Shield.

Torak plucked a twig from the mask's thorny mane and sniffed. 'Juniper. Fresh.'

'That has to mean there are places where the trees are still alive.'

'Mm. If so, the Deep Forest clans will want to keep them to themselves.'

She looked at him. 'Even now, after what's happened?'

''Specially now. You remember what they were like.'

Oh, she remembered.

The Deep Forest was different. The trees mistrusted strangers, it was easier to get lost – and its people were different too. At best they discouraged others from venturing in, and in the past they'd killed them. Their greatest wish was to be like trees. Thus they avoided speech, talking mostly with their hands, and woke fire only from wood, scorning others for using stone.

Renn pictured the Forest Horse Clan, who tattooed their faces with leaves and stained their lips and hair green. The Aurochs, who scarred themselves to look like bark. What she'd found most frightening was their ferocious conviction that theirs was the only True Way: that other people were less than human, and deserved to be killed.

Torak was eyeing the face on the rock and scratching the scrape on his cheek. Renn stopped his hand with hers. Brusquely he pushed her away: 'Leave me alone!'

She stared at him.

'Sorry,' he muttered, giving her that awful stretched grimace which had taken the place of his smile. 'Time to pitch camp. We'll have to stay out of sight.'

Watching him prowling about for a concealed campsite, she wanted to grab him by the shoulders and shout: What's wrong with you? How I can help if you won't *tell* me?

He'd changed so much since the Thunderstar. Prickly one moment, disturbingly absent the next. It was as if the Hidden People had stolen her Torak away and left this surly, haunted stranger.

At first she'd thought he was suffering from the sickness the clans call winter madness, which afflicts people and dogs in the Dark Time. But that was before the Walker. *He got too close to the trees...* Renn had her suspicions as to what this meant. But what was 'the black web'?

They camped in a snow-filled gully, Torak digging a snow cave and concealing it with branches. They woke no fire for fear of being seen, but they'd be warm enough. Fin-Kedinn had given Torak his reindeer-hide sleeping-sack, and Renn had Gaup's daughter's. Gaup was an old friend of Fin-Kedinn's and could be trusted to hold his tongue; his daughter never spoke.

Saving their pine-nuts and dried salmon cakes, they ate a cold, unpleasant nightmeal of gut mushrooms and winter frogstools: the colour of cloudberries, but tasting nothing like.

Before turning in, Renn drew lines of power around camp to ward off demons, using a little of her precious mix of earthblood and mammut ash. She'd wanted to dab some on Torak's forehead to stop him sleepwalking, but he was already curled up, pretending to be asleep.

A sharp east wind moaned through the gully. The sky was overcast. No snowglow, the darkness so thick she could touch it. With a shiver she stroked her clan-creature feathers. She pictured hostile clans creeping towards her. And demons, and faceless, soulless Skin-Takers…

Before the Thunderstar she would have snuggled against Torak in their double sleeping-sack and felt better. How was it possible that he could be so close, and yet here she was, aching with loneliness?

A cold nose touched her wrist. Wolf swung his tail. Rubbed his forehead against her hip.

Although Renn couldn't speak wolf talk, she understood what he was saying. *I am with you. We look after Tall Tailless together.*

Many Lights and Darks ago, the bad taillesses had stamped on Wolf's tail and it had made Wolf sick. Then Tall Tailless had chopped off the tip, and Wolf had got better. Now Tall Tailless was sick: a darkness inside, all happiness gone. But Wolf didn't know how to make him better.

Sometimes Tall Tailless was sad, sometimes angry, sometimes recklessly seeking danger. All Wolf could do was try to keep him safe.

Wolf was hungry too, and he missed his mate. If Darkfur had been with him they could have hunted together, but she wouldn't leave Pebble, who wouldn't leave his Den. So for now this was how it must be.

The brief Light had come and the taillesses were moving again, Wolf running ahead, then doubling back to make sure they were all right.

The ravens were cawing and peering down at him, waggling their tails to make him follow. Loping uphill, Wolf caught a distant tang of *living* trees... The muzzle-watering scents of grouse, squirrel, deer – and much closer, horse!

There. A shaggy black mare picking her way among fallen pines. Silently Wolf slunk after her, keeping into the wind so she wouldn't smell him.

The Bright Soft Cold was deep. It would be deepest at the bottom of the gully. Wolf decided to startle the mare into fleeing downhill, where she would flounder up to her belly...

The pack-sister appeared behind him, clutching her Long-Claw-that-Flies: she too had spotted the prey. But to Wolf's astonishment, she was waving her forepaws, *shooing the mare away*!

Flicking up her tail, the mare fled. Wolf hurtled after her. The mare was too crafty to get trapped in the drifts, she was veering *up*hill, leaping logs, clattering onto a frozen Fast Wet. Her hind hooves slipped, Wolf sprang at her rump, missed. The mare tail-slapped him stingingly across the muzzle and galloped off, spattering him with Bright Hard Cold.

Disgusted, Wolf shook himself and loped back to the taillesses. He stared at the pack-sister. She didn't even say sorry. Their first live prey in *ages* – and she'd *deliberately* spoilt the hunt! Some things about taillesses Wolf would never understand.

Tall Tailless hadn't noticed a thing. He was squatting on his haunches, peering intently at a line of shallow pits in the Bright Soft Cold. Tall Tailless did this a lot when he was hunting, Wolf didn't know why – although he'd noticed that often these pits smelt of prey.

This time they didn't. They smelt of the enemy of all wolves: *bear*.

'It's a bear den all right,' said Torak, peering inside the musty, well-trodden hollow between the giant roots of what had once been a spruce.

'Yes, and the bear might come back at any moment,' hissed Renn. 'We've got to get out of here!'

He didn't reply.

Dusk was falling, turning the snow blue. She tried to distract him by telling him about the mare. 'Just my luck it was one of the sacred black ones, so I couldn't shoot. But it *must* mean there's living Forest somewhere close!'

He wasn't listening. Wearing what she called his tracking face: dark brows drawn together, eyes remote, yet taking in every detail of what the snow was telling him.

To her consternation, he rose and started following the bear's tracks downhill. 'What are you doing?' she cried.

'It clawed this stump,' Torak said to himself. 'Hungry, bad-tempered…'

'Like me,' she snapped. 'Let's go before we bump into it!'

He was frowning, seeing the bear in his mind. 'It overturned this boulder, looking for grubs. This scat's two days old, mostly bark, must've eaten it to get its guts moving…' Stooping, he continued down the trail. Renn had no choice but to follow.

A bear is the strongest hunter in the Forest, and it can move in total silence. This one could be watching from two paces away and they'd never know until it was too late.

Renn took an arrow from her quiver. If *only* she had a better bow. Gaup's bow was ashwood strengthened with seal gut: hopelessly stiff, and it seemed to dislike its new owner. The feeling was mutual.

Below her Torak had quickened his pace. 'Here it scented prey – tracks are deeper where it jumped this log, raced after its quarry…'

'Torak, come *back*!'

'You said you were hungry! If it made a kill, let's see what's left.'

'*What? You can't take a bear's prey!*'

There are two rules for not getting killed by a bear. First: make a noise, so that it'll know you're coming and get out of the way. Second: never, *ever*, go near its kill.

Which was what Torak was trying to do right now.

Wolf was keeping close behind him, panting in alarm. Renn understood the glance he threw at her: *What's he doing?*

Torak halted. A few paces away from him, a boulder gleamed in moonlight. Beneath it lay the bear's kill.

The roe buck's carcass was alarmingly fresh, steam still rising from what remained of its belly. The bear had eaten its guts and bitten chunks out of its rump before kicking snow over what remained and wandering off.

Wolf's warning growl shook his whole body.

Renn's stomach clenched.

The bear hadn't wandered off, not at all. It was behind the boulder. Watching them.

Torak had seen it too. But to Renn's horror he drew his axe from his belt and strode *towards* the carcass. Towards the bear.

'*Torak, come back!*'

'Stay there,' he said over his shoulder.

EIGHT

With a startled pfui! the bear rose to its full height and stared at Torak.

'It's my kill now!' he yelled, brandishing his axe as he ran towards the carcass. 'Go away!'

The bear had never seen a human act like this. Dropping to all fours, it bounded off – then turned and gave an uncertain snort, sliding out its tongue to taste his scent. What *was* this creature who was trying to steal its kill?

'Go 'way!' bellowed Torak, grabbing the buck's leg and hacking at the joint. The flesh was frozen stiff, he couldn't cut through.

He was dimly aware of Wolf snarling, advancing on the bear, and Renn waving her axe and screaming. Soon it would realize he was bluffing. It would be on him in a single leap.

The hump of muscle between the bear's shoulders swayed as it shifted from side to side. One massive forepaw slapped the ground. It champed its jaws with a noise like rocks clashing. Baring its fangs, it roared. *That's MY kill! MINE!*

The last strip of hide snapped, Torak wrenched the haunch loose. *'Run!'* he shouted at Renn.

No one can outrun a bear, especially not in twilight down a snow-covered slope choked with fallen trees. Torak couldn't see Renn, she had to be somewhere below. He caught a blur as Wolf hurtled past, heading *up*hill, towards the bear.

Torak spun round to help. The bear was slashing at Wolf, who'd circled behind to distract it from his pack-brother. Torak saw Wolf dodge its claws, dart in, sink his teeth into its rump. The outraged bear gave a roar that shook the Forest. Again Wolf dodged the great claws that could gut him at a stroke. Now he was backing towards the carcass, snarling, goading the bear into following him to protect its kill. Wolf shot Torak a look: *Run!*

But Torak went after them, he couldn't leave his pack-brother. And yet if he attacked the bear with his axe, he might hit Wolf.

Uff! Wolf told him frantically. *Run!*

Again the bear turned on Torak. Again Wolf darted in to nip its rump. This time the bear ignored him, it was rocking from forepaw to forepaw, torn between the lust to tear Torak limb from limb and the urge to save its kill from this impudent wolf. Greed won: it galloped after Wolf. Torak saw his pack-brother racing uphill, the bear chasing at appalling speed.

Wolf leapt over the carcass and vanished into the dark. The bear roared, flinging branches, overturning boulders: *This is MY kill!*

The last Torak saw of it, it was prowling about the roe buck, huffing and clashing its jaws as it guarded its prize.

Torak breathed out. Savage laughter bubbled in his throat – and became a sob. He began to shake.

Flashes came at him from five winters ago. The demon bear erupting from the dark. His father lying dying in the wreck of the shelter, clutching his hand...

Torak swallowed hard.

Hoisting the buck's haunch on his shoulder, he started downhill to find Renn.

They pitched camp at the foot of the Shield, under a rocky overhang where boulders gave good cover. Torak decided to risk waking a small fire, and set the haunch to roast, having cut off the hock for Wolf, who'd returned, panting and bright-eyed after his encounter with the bear.

Renn tucked a piece of tendon under a rock as an offering to her clan guardian, then moved about gathering firewood. She hadn't spoken to Torak since he'd found her waiting stonily at the bottom of the hill.

When the silence had lasted long enough, he said: 'Come on, Renn. Don't be like this.'

She turned on him. 'Don't you *ever* do that again!'

'Look, I know I shouldn't have—'

'You could've been *killed*!'

'But I wasn't.'

'Stealing a bear's kill? Do you *want* to die?' She was trying to lift a branch that was too big for her and he made to help, but she warned him off with a glare; dropped the branch and stood with her hands on her hips, staring at nothing.

Though she was beyond the firelight, there was enough snowglow for Torak to see that she was trembling. He felt cold and sick. What have I done? he thought. He'd put her and Wolf in danger – and for what?

'Renn, I'm sorry, it was a stupid thing to do.'

'Yes, it was. Really, *really* stupid!'

'I don't know what came over me.'

'Don't you? I think you do! You've been different ever since the Thunderstar!'

He didn't reply.

Wolf had been watching them, ears and tail down as he glanced uncertainly from one to the other. He hated it when they fought.

'You've got to *tell* me,' said Renn.

Torak knelt and nuzzled Wolf's throat to say sorry for having put him in danger. They touched foreheads, Wolf wagging his tail and uttering low fervent whines, Torak clutching his scruff with both hands.

'Last autumn,' Renn went on, 'we promised each other: no more secrets.'

Torak gave Wolf the buck's hock and watched him lie down with it between his forepaws and start crunching it up. Torak didn't take his eyes off his pack-brother. He was aware of Renn coming to kneel beside him.

'Where are you, Torak?' she said sadly. 'I miss you. Where have you gone?'

He felt as if a lump of meat was stuck in his throat.

She took his hand. He gripped her fingers. 'I'm in the black web,' he said hoarsely. 'Burnt roots, branches... a horrible crackling. So much pain. The whole Forest gone, everything dead.'

'Maybe not everything. That spruce twig—'

'Look around you, Renn!'

'What about the Forest in the east? You saw it once from the Mountains, maybe it's all right! There's still hope!'

He heaved a sigh. 'I know that — but I can't *feel* it. Sometimes I can't feel anything, it's like the black web has set hard around me. Sometimes I feel too much, as if I'm missing a layer of skin, and everything hurts — Wolf wanting to play, the way you look at me.' He touched his ribs. 'And always this grief. This ache...' He broke off. 'I feel it all the time. I can't break free.'

She was staring at him aghast. 'So the bear... You went after its kill to break out of the black web?'

He nodded. 'Danger's the only thing that helps. And getting hurt.' He ground his knuckles against a rock.

'Don't.'

'Why not? I deserve it after risking your life.'

'No!' She pulled his hand from the rock. 'Oh, Torak. All this time you've been bearing it alone.'

'I didn't want to worry you.'

'You think I wasn't worried that you'd turned into a stranger?'

'Sorry.'

'Doesn't matter. You've told me now.'

The fire sputtered and spat. Renn adjusted the haunch of venison over the embers and said she had spruce bark and beard-moss in her medicine pouch, she'd make a poultice for his cheek. Her hair glinted red and gold like autumn leaves, and Torak knew how it would feel to run his fingers through it, to bury his face in the softness between her shoulder and neck and breathe her wonderful warm junipery scent.

He was amazed at how much better he felt for having told her. He hadn't realized what a burden it had been to keep the black web secret.

Wolf lay on his belly, demolishing the roe buck's hock. Torak watched Renn watching the embers, her dark eyes moving from side to side, as they did when she was deep in thought.

'The black web,' she said slowly. 'It's because you spirit walked in the Forest.'

He swallowed. 'I think so. Yes.'

'You got too close to the trees… And now the First Tree is gone, and the Forest is mortally wounded, so you're feeling its pain.'

It hadn't occurred to him that this might be linked to the First Tree. With her Mage's sense, Renn had seen further.

Frowning, she tested the venison with her knife. 'I wonder where the bear fits in.'

'It doesn't,' said Torak.

She shook her head. 'Until now you've always avoided bears.'

He snorted. 'Doesn't everyone?'

'Torak. You know what I mean. Your father.'

He pretended not to understand – but she was right. He could never see a bear in the Forest without thinking of Fa. And it was always Fa as he'd been that last night: the gash in his belly, his guts glistening in the firelight. The agony in his bloodshot eyes.

Wolf heaved himself to his feet and padded over to Torak, his warm gaze grazing his as he leant against him, shoulder to shoulder.

Renn took Torak's face between her hands and kissed his mouth. 'Wolf's right,' she told him. 'We'll find a way to make you better. Together.'

They broke camp soon after middle-night and started climbing a gully that seemed to lead to the top of the

Shield. From there they hoped to watch the sun peer over the Mountains for the first time in two moons.

A cold frosty night, brilliant with stars. As Torak followed Renn and Wolf up the gully he felt less troubled in spirit than he had since the Thunderstar. The previous Sunwake the Raven Clan had welcomed the sun by feasting on honeycombs. They'd woken a huge fire on a hilltop and shot arrows at the sky. He wondered what Fin-Kedinn and Dark were doing now.

Above him the strip of sky was slowly lightening. Rip and Rek swept overhead, cawing excitedly. The wind had dropped. It too was waiting for the sun to emerge from its cave.

Renn, toiling up the slope, came to an abrupt halt. 'Did you hear that?'

'Hear what?'

'I think – I heard a *jay!*'

They listened. Yes: from the other side of the Shield, a distant rattling call. Renn gave an incredulous laugh. 'Definitely a jay! Oh, Torak, surely that means living trees?'

He didn't reply. In the gathering light he'd spotted bird prints in the snow: willow grouse in their feathery snowshoes. 'Tracks!' he cried. 'And over there, fox – and hare, and snow-vole! They're fresh!'

Higher up they came upon an elk trail. 'These droppings are less than a day old,' said Torak.

Renn's face was alight with excitement. 'It was making for the top of the Shield, that has to be a good sign!'

From then on they kept to the elk's hoof-prints, which made climbing much easier. They passed a frozen waterfall hung with icicles longer than spears. Again heard the jay's raucous voice – and also the high-pitched calls of jackdaws greeting the dawn.

At last they reached the top of the Shield, where Wolf stood waiting in a cloud of frosty breath.

They couldn't see the land spread below as it was still in the shadow of the Mountains – but the sky above the snow-topped peaks was tinged with red. As Torak and Renn stood watching, this intensified to searing crimson ... expanding, brightening to orange... a silent explosion of dazzling brilliance – and suddenly there was the great blazing rim of the sun, warming their faces, turning the snow to glittering gold.

With a whoop, Renn shot an arrow in the air. Torak was grinning from ear to ear. Until now he hadn't quite believed he would ever see the sun again.

'Oh, Torak, *look!*'

Behind them the Dead Lands were an immense black wedge ravaged by the Thunderstar – but *before* them, sunlight was flooding a land that glowed with life. The Shield had been true to its name: it had protected the entire southern half of the Deep Forest. Torak saw valley after tree-covered valley – pine, spruce, oak, rowan, birch – all standing tall and proud and *alive* in their wintry mantles of sun-spangled snow.

Renn was laughing and kicking up flurries of shimmering

flakes, Wolf prancing around her in a joyful, rocking gait. 'I *knew* it!' she cried. '*Nothing* can destroy the Forest! Oh, Torak, I've missed it so much! And the *colours*! Those golden larches, the green green pines!'

His smile froze. He seemed to be seeing her through a speckly haze. Her voice reached him amid a harsh crackling of branches.

From his medicine pouch he brought out the lump of green amber and stared at it. He threw it away.

Renn noticed his expression. 'What's wrong?'

He looked at her. 'The trees, Renn. I can see that they're alive, but... I can't see the green. To me they're all just black.'

NINE

Renn knows it's a dream, but she can't wake up. She is in the ice cave at the Edge of the World, trapped in its freezing unearthly blue glow.

Naiginn is standing over her. Her half-brother: an ice demon in the form of a handsome young man. He knows no right or wrong, only the raging hunger to destroy – but he too is trapped, his demon souls sealed within mortal flesh by their mother's spell.

'You're going to set me free,' he tells Renn.

She can't move, can't make her lips say no.

'Oh, you will.' In the frozen light his mouth is blue as midnight, his skin as livid as death.

In his hands he grips the carcass of a newborn seal.

Without taking his eyes from Renn's, he twists off its head and feeds: sucking the brains, slurping the last smears inside the skull. Baring his teeth, he grins. 'Brains taste of souls, but I want the souls themselves. And for that I need to eat them alive.'

Panic squeezes Renn's ribs. Torak lies at Naiginn's feet. Next to him, Fin-Kedinn and Dark. Their bodies are frozen in ice, only their heads poking out, necks exposed to the knife Naiginn grips as he squats beside them.

His eyes are empty, cold beyond imagining. 'Which one shall I eat first? You choose. *Sister.*'

Terror overwhelming. She's trying to scream, can't make a sound except a dreadful straining wheeze...

'Renn, wake up!' Torak was shaking her. 'It's all right, you're safe!'

It took time to sink in. To smell her reindeer-hide sleeping-sack, to feel his arms holding her tight.

'Were you dreaming of him?' he whispered.

She nodded.

'He's dead. He can't hurt you any more.' Torak didn't speak Naiginn's name because clan law forbids naming the dead for five winters. Renn didn't name him because she feared that Naiginn was still alive.

Last autumn her mother had come to her in a dream. *You never saw the body... Are you sure he's dead? I told you it isn't over...* Renn had meant to tell Torak, but there'd never been a good time. Besides, what if the dream was merely another of her mother's tricks?

81

And now Torak was dealing with his own nightmare, the black web. One of the things Renn loved in him was his curiosity about how other creatures felt, but since the Thunderstar that gift had turned against him: he was feeling the Forest's anguish as no one else could.

It struck her as horrible that although he could no longer see green, she was seeing colour where she didn't want to. In her dream, everything had been intensely, dreadfully blue.

And the dreams in which she saw colours were the ones that came true.

Rip and Rek had a new trick: alighting on a branch and showering Renn with snow. She wished they'd get bored and fly away.

The dream had stayed with her, so to shake it off she'd slipped out at dawn for a few moments alone with her borrowed bow – having smeared ash on her skin to mask her scent and padded her quiver with moss to stop the arrows rattling.

It was good to be among living trees again. Goldcrests flickering among the pines, the snow criss-crossed with the trails of many creatures: badgers, squirrels, the deep dragging hoof-prints of aurochs – a calf's small ones printed inside those of its mother. Renn felt the dream wash away like a dark stain.

A hare paused at a hazel bush to nibble bark. Renn took aim. Missed. Tried again. Same result. *Wretched* bow. As for the arrows... how could you hit anything with gull-feather fletching and heron-bill points?

Finally she shot a willow grouse. By then she was so frustrated she nearly forgot to thank the bird and bid its spirit go in peace.

Back at camp, Torak greeted her with a nod that told her he didn't want to talk about the black web. She decided against telling him about Naiginn – at least, not yet. After all, it was only a suspicion. He must be dead. She and Torak had heard him scream...

They roasted the grouse, ensuring they kept the Pact by giving what they couldn't eat to Wolf and the ravens. 'How's the bow?' Torak asked.

Renn shuddered. 'Salmon Clan should stick to fishing. I couldn't hit a reindeer at two paces.'

He laughed. It was his first genuine laugh since the Thunderstar. Their eyes met. A current of heat coursed between them. They kissed.

'I've missed you,' said Renn.

'I'm sorry.'

They had camped on the Shield's southern flank, and planned to follow a frozen brook which should lead them down to the Windriver.

The snow was deeper here, and Torak had made snowshoes, stringing willow withes over loops of yew, which they tied across their toes with more withes, leaving the heels flapping loose. He went ahead to break the trail, Renn following in his tracks, Wolf weaving between the trees at his floating trot that seemed scarcely to touch the ground.

Torak gave a warning uff! and Wolf swerved to avoid something Renn couldn't see. 'Reindeer pit,' said Torak.

The pit was as deep as he was tall, lined with stones and hidden beneath a tracery of branches. Open Forest hunters dug similar pits, but they always warned people by leaving a twist of bark on a stick. Clearly, Deep Forest clans did not.

It was the only sign of people since they'd crossed the Shield, but they soon found tracks: long, narrow, stick-like, with small holes on either side.

'Fin-Kedinn warned me about these,' said Torak. 'They're like skates but longer, Deep Forest clans use them in snow. They stick fur on the undersides. The fur points backwards: makes you go faster downhill, grips the snow when you're climbing uphill.'

An east wind blew spindrift in Renn's face, making her shiver. It was noon, and around her the beech trees cast no shadow. They ought to be asleep, but she sensed that they were wide awake, watching these strangers in their midst. She wondered what else was watching.

Later they encountered the angry red glare of another clay mask. It was the same as the one at the Jaws of the Deep Forest, except for a sign gouged on its brow: the five-clawed print of a bear.

'By now they must know we're here,' Torak said quietly. 'Maybe they don't see us as a threat.'

He threw her a look. That had not been their experience of Deep Forest clans.

She said: 'I think from now on we should cover our tracks.'

'Wish we'd thought of it sooner.' He cut juniper boughs, handed one to her.

The brief winter's day was already dying. Wolf was restless, glancing often at Torak. The zigzag tattoos on Renn's wrists began to prickle.

Rip and Rek were uttering sharp calls that meant they'd found a carcass. So had a flock of crows. At Wolf's approach they flew off in a clatter of wings.

Not much left but skin and bones: a bull auroch, two females and a calf, in a broken huddle at the foot of a ridge. The calf's body looked frail beside the others. Renn remembered its small tracks printed inside those of its mother.

'Something panicked them over the edge,' said Torak.

'Wolverines sometimes stampede reindeer. But no auroch is scared of a wolverine.'

'And no human hunter would break the Pact by leaving carcasses untouched.'

He spotted something else: a stand of birch trees a few paces away, bark hanging in tatters from their trunks. The bark had been ripped off all the way round, killing the trees.

'Who would *do* this?' said Renn. 'No one kills a tree without reason!'

'Whatever clawed these trees wasn't human.'

She looked at him. 'Bear? Demon? ...Skin-Taker?'

'Whatever it was, it covered its tracks.'

Dusk was falling, they ought to pitch camp, but Torak was heading deeper into the trees. He beckoned to her.

A grove of ancient oaks, their twisted arms clotted with mistletoe. Rip and Rek perched in one gnarled giant with a hollow trunk. Wolf stood tensely watching.

Renn's hand went to her clan-creature feathers. 'A Death Tree,' she said softly.

Torak was moving towards it.

'Stay back!' she warned. The souls might still be around, angry and confused. They might try to possess him.

It was the way of all clans to leave their dead for other creatures to feed upon, but everyone differed in how they did this. In the Open Forest they left the body on a Death Platform facing upriver – so that, like the salmon, the souls could find their way to the Mountains and thence to the First Tree. Sea clans towed the corpse in a skinboat which they then sank, entrusting their dead to the Sea Mother.

Renn couldn't remember what Deep Forest people did, except that they placed the corpse inside a hollow tree. Torak's mother had been Red Deer: her Death Tree had been the Great Yew in the sacred grove. Maybe that was why he was peering inside the oak's trunk.

His voice echoed: 'From the tattoos, I'd say Bat Clan.'

'Don't touch!'

'I'm not. Come and look at this.'

She'd been a woman of about fifty summers. Plump, her face creased with laughter lines. Dead since before the Thunderstar, though as it was winter she didn't smell too bad. Torak was right about her clan-tattoo: a spiny black wedge on her chin, like the wing of a bat.

She'd been loved. Her kin had dressed her in a new parka and leggings of white winter hare fur and put her to rest with care, wedging her upside down inside the tree, in the same way as her clan-creature hung by its claws to sleep. They'd cut up her boots and scattered the pieces, so that she couldn't come back.

As she had once fed on Forest creatures, so now they had fed on her. Something had clawed open her belly and pecked out her eyes. This was as it should be. It wasn't what made Torak summon Renn.

He pointed at the dead woman's brow, then her breastbone. Renn sucked in her breath. 'No Death Marks!'

'Skin's been sliced clean away. I can't see from here, but I'd guess she's also missing them from her heels.'

No matter what clan you were, you *always* put Death Marks on a corpse: on the forehead for the world-soul, on the chest for the clan-soul, and on the heels for the name-soul. Death Marks kept the spirit intact on its journey. They stopped it turning into a demon or a ghost.

Renn was peering at the belly. 'Looks like a bear did this.'

Torak plucked a coarse hair. 'It's bear all right. But bears don't cut off Death Marks before they feed.'

Wolf's hackles were up. Renn's tattoos were still prickling. 'What does he smell?'

Torak glanced at his pack-brother, wordless speech passing between them. 'Bear. Says it's long gone.' He frowned. 'Tracks I found *look* like bear, but they're not.'

'What do you mean?'

'Can't put my finger on it, I just know they're wrong.'

Snow slid off a branch with a hiss, making them jump.

'Whatever cut out these Death Marks,' he added, 'it wasn't a bear.'

Renn nodded slowly. 'Edges are too clean.'

They looked at each other, remembering the dark tales at the clan meet: *People call them Skin-Takers...* They pictured shadowy creatures cutting away the Death Marks from the corpse before them, bending misshapen heads to feed...

Renn felt anger rising inside her. This woman had been someone's daughter, friend, mate, mother: under her moon-bleed tattoo were two dots, that meant two children. Her wristband had been clumsily plaited by childish fingers, maybe a grandchild. She hadn't deserved to be desecrated, her spirit endangered.

Wrenching off her mittens, Renn took a chunk of earthblood from her medicine pouch.

'What are you doing?' said Torak.

'Replacing her Death Marks. Her souls might still be near enough for it to work.'

Using her left hand, protected by her buckskin finger-guard, she drew red-brown circles on the frozen brow and breastbone. Torak lifted her so that she could reach the heels.

After that she put both fists to her chest and bowed to the corpse. 'May your guardian fly with you. May your souls stay together and find peace.'

They couldn't camp near the Death Tree, so they pressed on. A frosty night, Wolf's eyes silver in moonlight, but Torak smelt snow in the air and there was a ring around what remained of the moon. That meant a storm: the moon was warning all creatures to stay snug in their burrows.

He sensed something else too. These trees around him – oak, beech, lime – they should be asleep. Instead they were awake, brooding on the destruction of their sisters beyond the Shield. This part of the Deep Forest might have survived the Thunderstar, but it had not escaped unharmed.

Fallen pines blocked their way, forcing a detour. Ahead, a frozen lake glowed blue beneath shifting layers of smoke-frost. Torak made out the snowy mound of a beaver den. He tried not to think of the family of beavers that had been swept away...

They started across, keeping to the solid white ice and avoiding newer patches of treacherous grey.

'I feel eyes on us,' whispered Renn. 'D'you think someone saw us at the Death Tree?'

'If they did, we'd know by now.'

He could see no one on the surrounding slopes, only moonlit snow and tall black pines. But that meant nothing, Deep Forest clans were supremely good at concealment.

Wolf was sniffing the beaver den. Flattening his ears, backing away. A beaver trap? wondered Torak.

He was right. Not far from the den, a hunter had chopped a trench in the ice and laid a stick across it with snares hanging in the water. No need for bait. If a beaver woke up and swam out to its stores for a nibble of bark, it would spot the horsehair loops and investigate.

Again Torak scanned the slopes. The trap was recently made: the water hadn't had time to freeze.

Renn was moving off, Wolf at her heels with his nose to the ice. Something in his stance made Torak hurry to catch up.

Without warning Wolf threw himself at Renn, knocking her sideways.

'Renn, stay where you are!' cried Torak.

The beaver trap had been a decoy. This second trap was lethal: a large stretch of new ice hidden beneath the thinnest sprinkling of snow. One step further and she'd have fallen in, her clothes dragging her under to her death.

She shook her head in disbelief. 'This can't have been meant for prey, they'd never retrieve the carcass!'

Suddenly Torak was furious. 'What do you *want?*' he shouted at the silent slopes. 'We haven't done anything wrong!'

Wrong, wrong, echoed the hills.

'We've got to get off this lake,' said Renn.

She was right, they were too exposed.

Movement behind Torak. The pines on the slopes were shifting, sliding onto the ice. No, not pines, *hunters* in black-and-white parkas, raising spears, gliding down the banks on long narrow skates, speeding towards them.

Wolf was loping for a ravine on the nearer shore. Renn had torn off her snowshoes and was running after him. Kicking his feet free, Torak followed.

The ravine was choked with birches, he couldn't see Renn or Wolf.

A hand grasped his wrist and yanked him into the thicket.

'This way!' hissed a voice in his ear.

TEN

The blizzard was savaging the shelter, each fresh onslaught making the roof-tree groan and the reindeer-hide walls flap in and out.

Renn, shivering over an inadequate fire of elk droppings, pictured Bat Clan spears slashing their way inside. 'Are you sure they won't come after us?' she asked the woman who was both Leader and Mage of the Red Deer Clan.

'That was merely a warning,' muttered Durrain. 'If they'd wanted to kill you you'd be dead.'

'What did we do wrong?' said Torak.

'You were heading east of the lake.'

'We have to,' said Renn. 'We have to reach the sacred grove and do a Rite to bring back the First Tree.'

To her surprise, Durrain gave a weary shrug. 'You can't. It's against the rules.' She hadn't stirred from her place by the central tree-trunk since Torak and Renn crawled into the shelter. She sat cross-legged, twisting skeletal hands and peering through lank hair. Like the others huddled within, she was smeared from head to foot in ash. Guvach, the boy who'd found them, had explained that they were mourning their sisters: the trees in the Dead Lands beyond the Shield.

'What are these rules?' Torak said with a frown.

Durrain did not reply. It was Guvach who spoke. 'As long as we keep north of the Windriver, and west of the lake, *and* give them half our prey, they let us stay.'

'Who are "they"?' said Renn.

'You understand *nothing*,' said Durrain. 'We who were north of the Shield when the Thunderstar struck *deserve* to be punished! The Thunderstar wiped out the Lynx Clan, it killed half my people! It was the will of the World Spirit! Therefore it *must* be good!'

Good? wondered Renn. How could that be? And why had the Red Deer changed so much?

This was the clan which built magnificent shelters and wore fine clothes of nettlestem and elk hide; which kept aloof from others, never deigning to fight, trusting only in Magecraft and prayer. Renn used to find their sense of superiority irritating. If it hadn't been for the small black cloven hoof tattooed on each brow, she wouldn't have recognized these ragged, defeated people as Red Deer.

But why were they living like this? Eating bitter birch-bark gruel and wood-ant grubs, when there was prey in the Forest? Huddling over the feeblest of fires when they could have collected armfuls of wood?

Come to that, why had they built their shelter around a living pine that might easily be toppled by the storm?

The greatest change was in Durrain herself. Her eyes, once bright as beechnuts, were as filmy as those of a dead fish.

Only Guvach seemed to have a spark of spirit left. His ugly, genial face was covered in bumps like a toad's. His shrewd brown eyes missed nothing.

Torak said: 'Fin-Kedinn's camped with survivors on the Crowwater. We need to get word to him that there's unburnt Forest here—'

'I told you,' retorted Durrain, 'we're not allowed to leave. We have to obey the Chosen Ones!'

'The Chosen Ones?' said Torak and Renn together.

'Those who were south of the Shield when it struck,' Durrain said wearily.

'You mean the Bat Clan?' said Renn.

'And the Aurochs,' Guvach put in. 'And the Forest Horses.'

The Red Deer Mage was rocking back and forth. 'None of them were harmed by the Thunderstar... *Their* Leader kept them safe. They are indeed the Chosen Ones.' She heaved a sigh. 'It's right that they've forbidden Magecraft. What use was I?'

Renn stared at her. Magecraft, forbidden? She'd never heard of any clan doing without Magecraft…

Guvach said: 'The Leader of the Chosen Ones wields enormous power. He protected his people from the Thunderstar, and now he's keeping them safe from the Skin-Takers.'

As he spoke the name, people whimpered and mothers covered their children's ears.

'What *is* a Skin-Taker?' said Renn.

Guvach licked his lips. 'Some say they crawled from the swamp after the Thunderstar struck,' he whispered. 'They had no bodies till they took human form. Any stranger could be one. Only reason I knew you weren't was because I remembered you from three summers ago.'

'What do they want?' said Torak.

'To do evil!' He leant closer. 'They have icy wind for breath and they come when the moon is dark. They eat the dead, the dying, the helpless. Nothing can stop them. Anyone who ventures outside is lost.'

A gust shook the shelter, making Renn start. The walls were billowing, the pine tree groaning.

Torak looked from Guvach to Durrain: 'But you don't *have* to stay here! You could leave and join Fin-Kedinn!'

Durrain glowered at him. 'Who are you to tell us what to do? You come here breaking the rules, disrespecting the Forest with your seal-hide clothes! Can't you understand? The Thunderstar, the Skin-Takers – they are the will of the World Spirit!'

'A disaster that kills innocent people?' exploded Renn. 'Trees, prey, wolf cubs who never did anything wrong?'

'All is good, *all*!' repeated the Red Deer Mage. 'The First Tree is never coming back. Soon what's left of the Forest will die. We must *submit* – for what little time remains!'

For a moment no one spoke.

'The Leader of the Chosen Ones will protect us,' Guvach said uncertainly. 'So long as we obey his rules.'

Renn was about to protest, but Torak shook his head. This was getting nowhere.

Later, she lay beside him in her sleeping-sack. Out in the Forest the pines were roaring, the snowstorm redoubling its fury. Renn was exhausted but wide awake, picturing soulless creatures lurching through the dark.

In the past when she'd camped with the Red Deer Clan she'd felt secure, knowing herself protected by the best Magecraft in the Forest. Now Durrain had left the shelter open to attack. The clan had dogs, but they'd be no use, because like all Deep Forest dogs they were bred to silence and trained not to bark. And what was worse, Durrain had set no lines of power around the camp, not even a smear of earthblood over the entrance.

With a shiver Renn realized that the only thing between her and the haunted darkness was a single thickness of frozen hide.

Something struck the roof of the shelter and Torak jolted awake.

Above him through the smoke-hole he caught a gleam of eyes. Rip was perched on the edge, peering down at him.

The blizzard had gone off to savage somewhere else, and the wind had dropped to a moan. The fire was dead. The shelter was chilly. It smelt of dirty, frightened people.

Torak and Renn had unrolled their sleeping-sacks by the central pine, but Renn wasn't in hers. She was quietly stepping over sleepers, daubing lines of power on the walls while touching her belt and mouthing a charm.

She'd made the belt last autumn, out of Torak's old jerkin. From it she'd hung a deer hoof, a white pebble for the moon, one of Dark's slate frogs, and a woodpecker beak for piercing mysteries – spacing them widely, so they didn't rattle when she was hunting. She looked intent and assured. Torak envied her. Since the Thunderstar he even doubted his ability to track.

Guvach was also awake. Torak crawled over to him. 'We need to get word to Fin-Kedinn,' he said quietly. 'You could do it, Guvach. Tell him the Forest still exists.'

The bumpy forehead creased in confusion. 'But Durrain—'

'It's the right thing to do. Surely you can see that?'

The boy hesitated. 'Is it true you can talk to wolves?' he said suddenly.

'What's that got to—'

'Before the Thunderstar, Durrain foretold that a wolf might save the Forest. That has to mean something!'

Torak snorted. 'Mages' prophecies have a way of saying one thing and meaning another.'

Guvach's brows drew together. He picked at a scab on his thumb. 'They say you've spirit walked in trees... Heard the Voice of the Forest. You could spirit walk now. You could ask the Forest to call back the First Tree!'

Torak stared at him. 'You don't know what you're asking. Yes, I heard the Voice of the Forest, but for only an instant! Any longer and it would've torn my souls apart! And even if I tried, I'd be swallowed like a spark in a wildfire—'

'But the Chosen Ones will never let you near the sacred grove!'

'Maybe, but we have to try. And you have to get word to Fin-Kedinn.'

Guvach turned away. 'I told you, I can't.' He crawled back to his sleeping-sack.

Renn had been crouching nearby, softly blowing protective charms over the sleepers with her mammut-bone flute. Catching Torak's eye, she raised her eyebrows: *What was that about?*

He shook his head.

The wind had died. The hush was broken only by snores and slumbering breath. Through the smoke-hole the stars were distant and cold. *The First Tree is never coming back*, Durrain had declared. *Soon what's left of the Forest will die.*

Was she right? How could the whole Forest die? How could the First Tree have abandoned them?

Some of Torak's earliest memories were of gazing up at its rippling green lights. Snuggled by the fire, listening to Fa telling how its roots kept demons in the Otherworld, its boughs sheltered the clans on long winter nights when the Sky Bear had gobbled up the moon...

And now everything depended on this impossible Rite. And the moon was already in its last quarter, only days to go, and they hadn't found even one of the stones for the four arrows. What if Guvach was right, and the only hope was to spirit walk in the Forest?

Torak had never forgotten hearing the Voice. He dreaded hearing it again – and he longed for it. To be one with the trees. Even if it led to oblivion...

Outside, the dogs were whining almost inaudibly. Dog talk is like wolf talk, but simpler. Torak knew at once that they were afraid. Something was coming.

Renn lowered her flute. Her face was taut, listening.

A faint whistling sound, coming closer. It receded – then came closer again.

Durrain had woken. She sat rigid on the other side of the embers, clutching her knees.

Guvach was panting, his eyes starting from his head.

The hairs on Torak's arms were prickling.

A low, unearthly, whistling roar – growing louder, then fainter, then louder again, rhythmically like a pulse – but always coming closer.

The dogs were keening in terror. The whole shelter was awake, faces glistening with sweat.

Guvach stared at Torak. *Skin-Takers*, he mouthed.

Abruptly the dogs fell silent.

Torak heard footsteps in the snow limping towards the shelter. A heavy, irregular, dragging tread.

Renn had moved to huddle against him. He gripped her hand. Her fingers were cold.

The footsteps crunched nearer. Halted. Unbearably close. A foul, swampy smell wafted through the shelter.

On the side nearest Torak and Renn, the hide wall creaked, bowing inwards as something pressed against it.

Wrenching her hand from Torak's, Renn crawled towards it. Spreading her palms on the hide, she pressed back, hissing a charm.

A harsh exhalation of breath, brutal as a blow. Renn recoiled as if she'd been struck.

A thud shook the shelter. And another – on the opposite wall. People were moaning, children crying. More blows shaking the hides on all sides…

Suddenly they stopped.

More footsteps. This time heading away.

Again that unnatural, whistling roar. Growing fainter as the Skin-Takers lurched into the dark.

ELEVEN

L *ook at this.* Torak motioned to Renn.

She drew nearer, wincing at the crunch of her snowshoes. Overnight the snow had frozen to a brittle crust. It felt as if the Deep Forest was deliberately making things harder.

And now this: a pine cone wedged in the fork of a juniper. At first glance it appeared to have been left by a squirrel or a woodpecker; but it had been deliberately placed pointing right, and three scales had been cut out.

Sure enough, Torak took three paces along the elk trail they'd been following and spotted the trap, hidden in snow-covered undergrowth to his right. A cord of whitened sinew stretched at chest height, a sapling bent backwards – and secured to its crown, a fire-hardened spike. If he hadn't noticed the trap-marker, that spike would now be embedded in his chest.

'That's the fifth so far,' said Renn.

'And none of them aimed at prey.' Angrily he made to disable the trap. She stopped him.

'Do that and they'll know we're here.'

He ground his teeth. Why hadn't he thought of that?

She touched his shoulder. 'You all right?'

'Fine,' he lied. The ache under his ribs was worse, dragging him towards the sacred grove.

Two days since the visitation of the Skin-Takers. They hadn't come again, yet the threat was ever present. The morning after, Torak had searched for tracks, but found nothing, except for bloody smears where the dogs had been. If only he'd been braver. If he'd had the courage to venture outside, they might still be alive...

Durrain had withdrawn deeper into herself, sitting motionless by the roof-tree; but Renn's protective charms had impressed Guvach and his friends, and behind their Leader's back they'd equipped Torak and Renn for their journey.

The lengthiest part had been disguising them as Chosen Ones: binding their leggings and boots cross-wise with strips of whitened rawhide, making wovenstem bands to cover their noses and mouths, so as to conceal their smoky breath – and finally daubing them all over with a sticky blend of ash, chalk and tallow, and drawing charcoal stripes down their faces and clothes.

When it was done, Guvach had wrinkled his nose. 'At a distance they might mistake you for one of them. Close up, not a chance.'

He'd also given them a small bag of dried mushrooms and a final warning: 'Stay away from Death Trees,'specially if the head of the corpse has been eaten. Skin-Takers go for the eyes, tongues, brains. We don't know why.'

Wolf had vanished into the Forest, they hadn't seen him since leaving the Red Deer at dawn. He hated Torak and Renn's disguise. He couldn't understand why they wanted to resemble what he called 'the White Taillesses'.

Torak hated it too. The chalk felt stiff on his skin, as if he was turning into a tree, and Renn's ashen hair and face had transformed her into a wraith of shadow and snow.

Unlike him, she'd flatly refused to let Guvach draw the Chosen One's bear-paw mark on her forehead. 'Last summer I dishonoured my clan by putting on the marks of another, I won't do that again. And why bears?' Guvach wouldn't say. He seemed unsettled at the mere mention of the creatures.

Pines murmured in the wind, sending snow pattering onto Torak's hood.

'You don't look like you,' Renn said softly.

'Neither do you.' Slipping off his mitten, he touched the corner of her mouth, where the freckle he loved was concealed. She gave him a lopsided smile, and was briefly herself again.

The Forest was quiet, except for the swish of raven wings and the hiss of snow slipping off branches. Thanks to Guvach they'd found the Windriver, but they had to stay off the ice for fear of being seen. They also had to brush out their tracks with juniper boughs, and watch for traps. Guvach's sister had tied ptarmigan feet to the heels of their snowshoes, because ptarmigans run fast over snow. It didn't seem to be working.

The next trap lay in plain sight at the foot of a spruce. It was very simple and very cruel: a lump of meat the size of a baby's fist, wrapped in a gleaming black band tied on with sinew.

'I've never seen anything like this,' said Renn.

'Neither have I, but I've heard of it. That strip's cut from the springy black plates some whales have instead of teeth. You sharpen both ends and soak it to make it supple, then wrap it round the bait, tie it in place with sinew. Prey swallows the bait, sinew dissolves in its belly and...' – with his knife Torak cut the sinew, and the whale bone sprang open. He indicated the spiked ends – '...both points straight through the guts.'

Renn was aghast. 'If anything swallowed that it could take days to die.'

Torak nodded. He'd heard of this evil from the White Foxes in the Far North, but no one used it now, it belonged to the bad times in the Great Cold. 'Who would carry whale bone in the Deep Forest?' he mused.

Warily, Renn touched the trap. Grimacing, she wiped her mittens in snow. 'Smeared with honey! It can't be meant for bears?'

'We passed a bear trail a while back.'

'But no one hunts bears, it's against clan law.'

'It's against clan law to hunt any hunter in the Forest. And yet any hunter could have gone for this: lynx, wolverine... Wolf.' Savagely he cut the whale bone to shreds and buried them.

The glitter had gone from the snow, shadows were turning violet. The clans called this the demon time, when they creep out of the murk, breathing malice and despair.

'We need to make camp,' said Renn.

Torak cast about. 'We could dig ourselves fox-holes among those limes,' he said doubtfully. 'Even without fire, our body heat would get us through the night.'

'And if they found us we'd be trapped.'

Deep Forest clans are like deer in that they seldom look up. Torak and Renn found an old oak that felt friendlier than most. Thick ropes of ivy clung to its trunk, making it easy to climb. They made a cold, fireless camp in the crux of its arms – having first said sorry to it with a speck of Renn's precious mammut ash.

They'd obliterated their tracks underneath, although Torak worried they might have shed bits of chalk. No ordinary hunter would spot these, especially at night. But Deep Forest people were extraordinarily observant.

It was snowing again. An owl shrieked. Her mate's shivering reply rang through the Forest. Torak hadn't seen Wolf since morning. He pictured whalebone traps laid temptingly in the open.

Renn's breath warmed his cheek. 'Wolf will be all right,' she whispered. 'He knows to avoid traps.'

But Torak had to be sure. He was about to call to his pack-brother when a wolf's howl echoed across the valley, then another and another. He lowered his hands. Those howls weren't Wolf.

By the sound of it the pack was a big one, eager to hunt. Torak pictured them howling with their eyes slitted and their muzzles all pointing the same way so as to intensify the echo and make them seem more numerous than they were. *We are many! Keep out!*

His spirits sank. First the Chosen Ones and the Skin-Takers, then that horrible trap – and now this pack of stranger wolves. He couldn't risk howling to Wolf, that might alert them to his presence. He could only stay silent and beg the Forest to keep his pack-brother safe.

If the stranger pack caught Wolf in its range, it would tear him to pieces.

Wolf went flying over the Bright Soft Cold. The stranger pack was gaining on him.

He was faster than the males but the females were lighter and swifter, especially the one in front, and she knew every step of her range. Wolf only knew that he had to keep off the frozen Fast Wet, or they would spot him in a snap.

A fallen tree blocked his path. Jutting branches made it impossible to leap so he scrambled underneath. The trunk was lower than he thought, he was stuck. He heard thudding paws, caught the lead female's furious scent. She snapped at his tail. He scrambled out from under and fled.

Turning on his forepaw, he put the wind at his rump and headed for an alder thicket. If he could hide in there he might throw her off the scent. If not he'd be trapped.

The Bright Soft Cold was deep, he floundered between tangled trees. The lead female wasn't following. Had she lost his scent? Or was she lying in wait?

He smelt tiny puffs of bird breath rising from a drift, swerved to avoid them: if he startled the grouse from their burrows they would give him away.

He came to a couple of sleeping reindeer dusted in Bright Soft Cold. With a startled grunt the mother lumbered to her feet, swiping at Wolf with her head-branches. A prong grazed his haunch, he stifled a yelp and ran on. He was nearly through the thicket.

It *had* been a trick: the lead female had raced round to the other side and was waiting for him, two sturdy young males flying to join the attack. Wolf shot past their noses and hurtled into a pine wood.

They were trying to chase him uphill, knowing that as he was bigger, he'd go slower than them. He veered *down*hill. A gully ahead, he hated narrow places, couldn't smell what lay in front. Shooting out the other end, he found himself slithering over boulders slick with Bright

Hard Cold, tumbling into a drift. He struggled free, loped on through the Dark.

The female wasn't following. Another ambush?

Suddenly he was running through torrents of fresh, powerful scent. Relief washed over him. The lead male had scent-marked trees, bushes, rocks along the edge of his range. Wolf sped past the border and into the next valley.

Behind him the stranger wolves were running up and down the edge of their range, panting and yelping. Their leader stood rigid, glaring at Wolf. Throwing up his muzzle, the lead wolf howled, threateningly deep: *Stay out of our range!*

Wolf slowed to a trot, flanks heaving, legs trembling with fatigue.

He smelt that he was in a part of the Forest that belonged to no pack. All packs had such places between their ranges, to prevent them killing each other by mistake. They were good places for a lone wolf to hide – and also to hunt, as prey often came here to avoid the packs.

Wolf thought with a pang of Darkfur and Pebble. Without him they were just two wolves struggling to hunt and protect their range. What if a stranger pack decided to attack?

Worrying about this, Wolf caught the scent of a bear carcass. He was hungry, but the carcass smelt so odd he didn't dare touch it, not even to roll in it to hide his scent.

Loneliness clawed his chest. He couldn't smell Tall Tailless or the pack-sister, they were many lopes away. And he couldn't howl in case he alerted more wolves.

Wolf *hated* this part of the Forest. The trees were awake when they should be asleep, and Tall Tailless and the pack-sister had changed their overpelts so that they smelt all wrong.

A new scent on the wind. Wolf recognized it at once: the fierce White Taillesses who'd attacked his pack-brother and -sister.

Next moment he saw them, directly ahead. He saw their Long-Claws-that-Fly poised to shoot. He smelt their uncertainty and fear.

All at once, the White Taillesses lowered their Long-Claws and put their forepaws to their chests: *they were bowing to him.* Now they were turning away, vanishing into the Dark.

Wolf was astonished. Why would White Taillesses hunt his pack-brother and the pack-sister – and yet bow to him?

Renn was chilly and cramped, huddled in her sleeping-sack and tied to a branch of the oak in case she fell in her sleep. Torak was also awake. She knew he was worrying about Wolf.

It had stopped snowing and the sky was clear, the night hushed except for the thin cries of redwings. The crescent moon was almost spent, no strength left to shed light.

Moving carefully so that her clothes made no noise, Renn peered into the darkness below. She dreaded seeing hunters smeared in charcoal and chalk stealing through the snow... Skin-Takers hauling themselves up the trunk...

Guvach's warning had been gnawing her all day. *Skin-Takers go for the eyes, tongues, brains...* What was she missing?

Then it came to her. Her dream: Naiginn sucking the brains of the newborn seal. What if her suspicions turned out to be true, and he *was* still alive and had found his way to the Deep Forest? What if he was using Skin-Takers to gather what he craved?

It would explain that whalebone trap. A cruel, slow means of killing would appeal to an ice demon. But how did bears fit in? Renn knew it made a pattern. She just couldn't see it.

The oak's branches shivered. Below her Renn saw a bison huffing in a mist of starlit breath. Grunting with pleasure, the great beast was giving its shoulder a luxuriant scratch against the trunk's rough bark.

Renn's belly rumbled. Torak's eyes gleamed. *I'm hungry too*, he mouthed. To save their provisions they'd eaten an unsatisfying nightmeal of beechnuts and frost-shrivelled rosehips.

Swinging its short tail, the bison ambled off.

Soon afterwards a Forest horse paused to rub her bristly mane against the oak. Raising her head, she gave Torak a penetrating look, then melted into the shadows.

Night wore on. Renn caught the glitter of frost-encrusted antlers. A reindeer was nibbling beard-moss off the oak's lower branches.

Torak's parka creaked as he leant towards her. 'I've been thinking about that trap,' he breathed. 'Whale bone's from the Sea, no Deep Forest clan would trade for it. Whoever set it has to be an outsider.'

'I think so too,' she whispered. Now was the time to tell him about Naiginn. 'There's something else I have to—'

He signed her to silence.

The reindeer was trotting off, tendons clicking. Torak pulled his wovenstem band over his mouth and nose. Renn did the same. 'I don't like this,' he murmured. 'All these creatures came from the same direction: they're moving away from something...' Suddenly his eyes widened.

Not daring to bend her head, Renn glanced down.

What appeared to be spindly black-and-white trees were stealing soundlessly out of the dark.

TWELVE

Holding their breath, Torak and Renn watched the Chosen Ones searching the ground beneath the oak. If any of the hunters glanced up, they'd be spotted in a heartbeat.

Some Chosen Ones were scrutinizing hoof-prints in the snow, some examining drops of frozen reindeer spit on branches. Dawn was breaking. They had no need of torches.

A hunter plucked a tuft of bison hair from the trunk. He threw it aside, peered at the bark. Renn prayed to her clan guardian that he hadn't spotted any scuff-marks she and Torak might have left as they climbed.

Two others had found something. Slipping off their mittens, they signed to the others, who converged as fast as eels at a drowning. Chalk-white fingers twisted in silent, jerky speech.

Drawing apart, the Chosen Ones intensified their search, moving noiselessly on long narrow snowshoes of polished bone. All were bristling with axes, spears, bows, thin slate knives. All were men, in white parkas and leggings striped with charcoal to blend in with the trees. The ruffs around their hoods were dog fur, which doesn't clog with frozen breath; Renn couldn't make out their clans till they drew back their hoods to listen.

The Forest Horses' hair and beards were braided and stiff with chalk. Where they'd licked it off their lips were green.

The Bats' hair was short as fur and blackened with pitch. The tips of their ears had been cut to mimic their clan-creature's pointed ears.

The Aurochs' earlobes were pierced with rolls of birch bark, their scalps and faces shaven and ridged with scars. Many clans gave themselves raised scars; Fin-Kedinn's were on his upper arms, he'd made them by slitting the skin and rubbing in lichen. But no one in the Open Forest carved their flesh all over to look like bark.

Renn became aware that Torak was frantically mouthing her name. With his eyes he indicated a flake of chalk on her knee: it was poised to fall off. She saved it just in time, but her movement loosed a sprinkling of snow. In horror she watched it drifting down towards the Chosen Ones...

Rip thudded onto a pine, and all heads turned towards him – away from the oak.

Torak rolled his eyes. *That was close!*

The raven's head-feathers were raised in two aggressive 'ears' and he was cawing angrily at the Chosen Ones. They acknowledged the bird with respectful nods. In her mind Renn begged Rip not to gurgle a greeting at her – or worse, fly onto her shoulder.

Rip coughed up a pellet, then uttered a rattling call. Rek's answer echoed through the trees. Hitching his wings, Rip flew off to join her.

Silently the Chosen Ones followed the raven's flight, then turned back to the oak. Renn and Torak stopped breathing. It was only a matter of time before they were detected.

And yet... The Chosen Ones seemed to have lost interest in the oak. They were gazing at a boulder some distance beyond.

Beside the boulder stood Wolf. His tail was high, his head imposingly raised. His snow-spangled fur blazed golden in the rising sun.

Renn and Torak exchanged terrified glances. *What's he doing?*

Wolf was wary of strangers, he rarely let them see him... Why now did he leap effortlessly onto the boulder and stand staring down at the Chosen Ones? His amber eyes were stern, unyielding. Renn knew enough wolf talk to know what they were saying: *Be gone!* With a shiver of awe, she remembered that Wolf had once hunted on the Mountain of the World Spirit.

The Chosen Ones too were awestruck. A Forest Horse

cut off the tip of his beard and laid it in the snow as an offering. An Auroch sliced open his palm and sprinkled blood. One by one, each man left a tribute for the great grey wolf.

Then, putting their fists to their chests, they bowed low, and disappeared into the Forest.

Huddled with Renn under a snow-bent spruce, Torak uttered three long howls: *Come – to – us!*

Black-and-white birches sparkled with hoarfrost. Overhead, Rip and Rek were sky-dancing. They were excellent watch-ravens, they would warn if there were Skin-Takers or Chosen Ones about.

One moment Torak was watching a squirrel leaping from branch to branch. The next, there was Wolf, bounding towards him through the trees, pouncing on him with a vigorous greeting.

Torak knew that his pack-brother had deliberately confronted the Chosen Ones to prevent them spotting him and Renn, and he couldn't let that happen again. What if next time the Chosen Ones weren't quite as awestruck? What if they glimpsed movement among the trees and shot Wolf by mistake?

How to explain this to him? Wolf talk involves your whole body, and as Torak only had two legs and no hackles or tail, he would never speak it as well as his pack-brother.

The White Taillesses are dangerous, he began.

Wolf's amber gaze grazed his, agreeing that this was so. *Stay away from them. They might hurt you… by mistake.*

Wolf rubbed his shoulder against Torak's, raising a puff of chalk. He sneezed. *But they hunt you and the pack-sister.*

Yes, but…

Wolf took Torak's upper arm in a gentle muzzle-grab. *Wolf keeps Tall Tailless and the pack-sister safe.*

Torak sighed. He tried again. Wolf still didn't understand. He failed to see why it mattered that the White Taillesses were dangerous. If they hunted members of his pack, he must risk his life to save them. It was as simple as that.

Wolf's whiskers tickled Torak's ear as he soft-nibbled under his jaw. *For many Lights and Darks, you're sad,* said Wolf.

Yes.

Why?

Torak hesitated. *The Forest is hurt. It's making me… sick.*

Why?

How to describe spirit walking in trees?

Once, Torak had spirit walked in an eagle. Wolf had been with him, but Torak wasn't sure if he'd realized what was happening: if he'd been aware that Torak's name-soul and clan-soul had been inside the eagle, so that he'd experienced flying as a bird, while his world-soul had remained in his unconscious body on the ground.

In the cold treeless lands, he began. *I flew in an eagle.*

Again Wolf rubbed against him.

Once I... I was tree. Now many trees are Not-Breath: bitten by the Great... the Great Beast-that-Bites-Hot from the Up.

Grunt-whining in puzzlement, Wolf padded in circles around Torak. He twitched his ears at the surrounding birches. *But these trees are alive.*

Seeing the puzzlement in the beloved furry face, Torak gave up. He couldn't tell whether his pack-brother was trying to make him feel better, or simply didn't understand. There would always be this distance between them, because Wolf was wolf and he was human. It made him feel lonelier than ever.

And he perceived anew the hopelessness of their task. They still had a long way to go to the sacred grove, through a Forest crawling with Chosen Ones, demons and Skin-Takers. They hadn't begun to find the stones for the four arrowheads, or to work out how to do the Rite. And when dusk fell, it would be the first night of the moon's dark.

'Does Wolf understand?' asked Renn.

'I don't think so.'

'Did you warn him about that trap?'

'He knows to avoid traps.' Spoken with more conviction than he felt. Wolf called traps Branches-that-Bite. His nose was so keen he could smell one in the next valley. Surely he would know to avoid any with whalebone spikes?

'I've been thinking about it,' Renn said in a low voice. She was chewing her lower lip, as she did when she was working up to tell him something she should have revealed sooner. It was so endearing that he couldn't help smiling. 'What is it?'

She sucked in her breath. 'I think I know who set that trap.'

'Naiginn's *alive?*' he repeated. 'But – how can that be? We heard him scream...' He was shaking his head, struggling to take it in.

To her relief he hadn't reproached her for not telling him sooner. He'd simply listened in incredulous silence, his light-grey eyes narrowing, as if reading tracks in the snow.

'It's the only thing that explains that trap,' she insisted.

Reluctantly he nodded. 'And – Deep Forest people might be weird, but they don't kill bears.' He paused. 'I just thought of something. Last summer the scar on my forearm itched when Naiginn was near. Same with the one on your hand. So if he's alive, why aren't they itching now?'

'I don't know.'

The wind was rising, the pines beginning to moan. The sky was heavy with snow.

Renn had been half-hoping that Torak would dismiss her suspicions, maybe provide some reason why Naiginn couldn't possibly be alive. The fact that he was even conceding it might be true made it horrifyingly real.

Last summer Naiginn had held her captive. To get what he wanted he would have maimed her as readily as gutting a fish. In her mind she pictured his handsome, unfeeling face, his empty ice demon stare.

Torak was running his thumb along his lower lip. To her alarm his reservations seemed to have been replaced by a kind of grim relish.

'You almost seem – pleased,' she said.

He looked at her. 'I never got the chance to beat him up for how he treated you.'

'And you won't now! Remember, you and he are—'

'Bone kin, yes, I know. But I've always hated that we never got to fight.'

'Keep it that way!'

His snort told her what he thought about that. 'But what's he doing in the Deep Forest?'

'Remember he liked head meat?'

He shot her a glance. 'You're thinking – that Death Tree?'

'I think he sends the Skin-Takers to find what he needs. But why aren't the Chosen Ones stopping him?'

'He told me once that as a boy he was fostered with the Aurochs and the Swans. Maybe they don't know what he is.'

She was nodding. 'And it explains how a boy from a treeless land knows to find his way around a forest.'

'Not as well as us,' snarled Torak.

Renn felt a shiver of foreboding. In his disguise Torak

looked disturbingly ruthless, the chalk and charcoal accentuating the strong planes of his face.

And she could tell that he was picturing exactly what he would do to Naiginn when he got the chance.

A bear had taken the bait, and Torak could see from the dark splinters in the snow that the trap had been the same as before: a lump of meat wrapped in sharpened whale bone and smeared with honey.

Wolf was off hunting and Renn had halted to re-tie her snowshoes. As Torak waited for her to catch up, he studied the trampled snow around the rocks.

At least he tried to. Three days since leaving the Red Deer camp, and the black web was making it hard to concentrate. Slipping off his mitten, he touched the bottom of the bear print. Frozen, and sprinkled with pine-needles where a deer had tugged moss from an overhanging branch. These prints were several days old.

In the lee of a boulder Torak found something else: the ghosts of a man's bootprints. His heart began knocking against his ribs. The man who'd made these tracks had had an odd walk, his left foot turned outwards. *Like a duck*, Torak had told Renn once, mocking Naiginn's walk.

Slowly he followed the trail. The bear had wandered into this gully. It had sharpened its claws on the trunk of this lime tree. It had splashed dark-yellow urine on that rock. Here it had clawed a hollow in the snow and curled up for a nap.

After that, everything had changed. The signs were so clear that not even the black web could stop Torak seeing it in his mind. The bear lurching to its feet, crashing against rocks, snapping saplings in its agony as the whalebone spikes pierced its guts.

He found the carcass behind more rocks – or rather, what Naiginn had left of it. The ice demon had cut off all four paws and skinned the rest. He'd also eaten the eyes and picked the skull clean. What remained was a pathetically scrawny carcass that looked almost human.

Again Torak removed his mitten. Placing his hand on the bloodied skull, he addressed the creature's spirit. 'Wherever you are, be at peace.' He was uncomfortably aware that he'd spoken out of duty, not compassion. He found it hard to feel pity for any of their kind after what a bear had done to Fa.

Bears were the mightiest hunters in the Forest, which was why the World Spirit had decreed there would never be a Bear Clan: its clan guardian would be too strong. Some clans feared naming the creatures out loud, instead calling them Honey-Eaters or Furred Ones. Everyone respected bears – but nobody trusted them, because bears live on their own, and if they get the chance, males eat their young.

None of which told Torak why Naiginn had slaughtered this bear so cruelly, then flayed and dismembered its carcass.

He was trying to work it out while cleaning his hands with snow when a knife jabbed under his chin and a cold voice spoke: 'Don't move, unbeliever.'

THIRTEEN

Dark cowered in total blackness, his strike-fire cold in his fist. He was back where he had told himself he would never go again, doing the one thing the Hidden People hated above all else: he was seeking them out.

It was the day after Torak and Renn had left for the sacred grove. He missed them. And his Mage's sense told him that they couldn't do the Rite without him.

Four arrows to bring back the First Tree, the Walker had said. *And they can't be ordinary stones, oh, no... Have to be bluest of blue and reddest of red, clearest of clear...*

Torak and Renn were seeking the green heartstone; as for the other three, Dark was convinced that only he knew where to find them: in the Cave of the Hidden People.

This was why he had ventured underground, groping his way to the balancing rock and belly-crawling through that impossibly low tunnel to reach their lair.

Now in the darkness he felt their anger beating at him in waves. 'I bring three gifts,' he told them. 'All I ask in return is three small pieces of crystal.'

Unyielding silence throbbed in his ears.

Shakily he struck a spark. His rushlight glimmered awake. He blinked in disbelief.

He *had* found his way to the cave of the crystals, he *knew* he had – but instead of its rainbow glitter, everywhere he turned he saw nothing but dank grey stone. The Hidden People had the power to make you see things which didn't exist – and they could also make things disappear.

While Dark had been living by himself in the Mountains, he'd learnt that when you're carving you have to think five cuts ahead. He'd done the same thing today as he'd made his way to this cave, leaving a rope in position at the balancing rock, and ensuring that he had his offerings readily to hand. With trembling fingers he laid them on the ground.

'Feather of my spirit guide, the white raven,' he declared to the listening silence.

A low humming at the edge of hearing. He felt the power of the Hidden People thrumming through him, like the beginning of an earthshake.

'A hair from the Deep Past...' He laid down the strand of mammut hair he'd extracted from the wristband Renn had given him last autumn.

The humming was growing more intense, their anger growing with it, stone dust trickling from the roof. The offerings weren't enough.

'I am a *Mage*!' he cried, striking the ground with the butt of his knife. 'I *will* be heard!'

Heard, heard... mocked the Hidden People. But the humming was receding, and no more stone dust fell.

'Take my offerings!' insisted Dark. 'Give me what I seek!'

The humming sank to nothing. He held his breath.

Into the silence dropped the sound of falling water.

Dimly, beyond his rushlight, he made out a stream where no stream had flowed before. Water was pouring over folds of pallid stone and pooling in a shallow basin, hollowed from the rock by unseen hands.

Dark hesitated. The Hidden People must be showing him this for a reason.

Heart thudding against his ribs, he cupped his palms and drank. The purest water he'd ever tasted: like drinking moonlight.

Dipping in his forefinger, he wetted his eyelids. When he opened his eyes, *he saw*.

The Hidden People were emerging from the floor, the walls; they were standing with their feet on the roof and their heads beside his, so that he could no longer tell up from down.

The men were tall and fierce, with eyes like shards of flint. The women were beautiful, with faces of glistening slate. When they turned their backs their spines were hollow and pitted as granite. One leant towards him, her breath chilling his skin as she teased his long locks of frost-bright hair through hard translucent fingers.

'I seek three stones for the Rite,' he gasped. 'In return I'll give you my third offering: the thing you desire above all else.'

She bared sharp teeth in an impenetrable smile. Then, as silently as they'd appeared, the Hidden People became one with the shadows. And still the stream flowed, its bubbling echoes filling the cave with the smell of water.

With a jolt Dark realized that both Ark's feather and the mammut hair were gone. In their place jutted two small fangs of bright crystal: one radiant scarlet, the other luminous blue.

He tried to pick them up. They were embedded in the rock. He'd brought his antler pick, but he knew that if he tried to hack them loose, he would never see daylight again.

Once more he spoke to the shadows. 'My third offering is this: above all things, you desire to be left alone. But if others find this cave – and they will – you'll never have peace again.'

The water fell silent. The stillness was absolute.

With his knife, Dark cut his palm. 'By my blood on this blade and by my three souls, I swear that if you give me these crystals, I will make sure you stay hidden for ever!'

A change in the air. Around him the rocks were buckling and stretching... Now the scarlet crystal and the blue lay loose upon the ground. Bowing his thanks, Dark put them in his pouch.

Dare he ask for more? 'I need the – the crystal clear as ice...' he stammered.

Harsh breath blew out his rushlight. The humming rose angrily.

'At least tell me how to find it!' he begged.

Find it, find it... taunted the Hidden People.

Somehow, Dark found the tunnel and belly-crawled through. Fumbling for the rope he'd looped around the support stone, he yanked with all his might, scrambling clear just as the balancing rock crashed down, sealing the cave for ever.

'I kept my word!' he shouted at the Hidden People. 'Tell me how to find the ice crystal!'

As he crawled to safety, a stony voice murmured in his mind: *The answer lies in the jaws of the wolf...*

Up on the ridge, Darkfur and Pebble gave him an affectionate greeting. Darkfur rose on her hind legs and rubbed noses, Pebble made rar-rar noises and pawed Dark's pouch to get at the stone creatures inside. But if they had anything to tell him about the ice crystal, they couldn't make him understand because he didn't speak wolf talk.

Pebble had recovered from his ordeal with a speed which would have astonished anyone who didn't know wolves.

His sore nose and pads had healed and his scorched fur was growing back thicker than ever. He had regained enough confidence to venture into the Dead Lands with his mother, although sudden noises still sent him bolting underground.

Seating himself on a boulder, Dark drew the two crystals from his pouch. They flashed and winked in the sun: one the clear scarlet of lingonberry juice, the other the lucent blue of a sunlit Sea. His fingers itched to be fashioning arrowheads for the Rite.

Two out of four, he thought. That left the ice crystal still to find, and the heartstone, whatever that was.

And there was even more to the arrows than that. Before the Walker had wandered off from camp, he had told Dark that each arrow must be made just so: the right wood for the shaft, the right sinew to bind it, the right feathers for the flights.

For a moment, Dark's spirits plunged. Even if he found the ice crystal and made the arrows – even if Torak and Renn found the heartstone at the sacred grove – how could he find *them* in time to do the Rite? In a few days it would be Sunwake, and soon after that, the dark of the moon...

Pebble was eyeing the crystals hopefully. Dark closed his fist, remembering the young wolf's liking for licking stones. *The answer lies in the jaws of the wolf...*

Pebble put his muzzle on Dark's knee. Swinging his tail, he glanced at Dark, then away.

With a sigh Dark scratched the young wolf's scruff. 'Torak should be here, not me. He'd understand what you're trying to say.'

On his way back to camp, Dark spotted a party of water-carriers returning from the caves with skins they'd been filling at the lake. His heart sank. They were Swans. His father was among them.

To avoid them, Dark ducked behind a shelter. It didn't work. Realvi left the group, dodged round the other side of the shelter and barred his way. 'I need to talk to you,' he said in a low voice.

'Get out of my way,' growled Dark.

'You can't keep avoiding me!'

'Yes, I can!'

Realvi grabbed his shoulder. Dark pushed him backwards into the snow.

People were staring. Shamik stood slack-jawed with Spike the hedgehog in her arms. Ark, perched on top of the shelter, half-spread her wings and ruffled her head-feathers in alarm.

Setting his teeth, Dark reached down and helped Realvi to his feet.

'I'm your father,' panted Realvi, brushing himself off. 'I have the right to talk to my son!'

'You gave up your rights,' retorted Dark, 'when you left me in the Mountains.'

His father flinched. 'But you can't deny who you are! We share the same clan-tattoos – same clan-creature skin – same marrow!'

129

'So what if we're the same clan?' Dark flung back. 'So what if I have this tattoo on my forehead, and this – ' he touched his swanhide wristband – 'and this – ' the feather tied to his hood. 'I can't change what I was born, but *no one* can tell me how to live!'

'Just *listen*, will you?' Realvi cast about to make sure they weren't overheard. 'Why d'you think I've been trying to talk to you ever since we got here? I'm trying to give you good news!' He leant closer. 'When the Thunderstar struck we were hunting in the Deep Forest. That's why we survived. *South of the Shield, the Forest is still alive!*'

Dark stared at him. He shook his head. 'If that was true, you'd have told us as soon as you got here!'

'I'm telling you now.'

'Why?'

His father's bony features twisted. 'I'm trying to make amends. I – I'm sorry for what I did all those winters ago. Sorry I abandoned you.'

Dark tried to swallow, but his throat had closed. There was a pressure inside his skull. He felt as if his head was going to burst.

'Dark—'

'What do you *want* from me?' he cried.

His father swallowed. 'Forgiveness.'

Dark pushed past him. 'Leave me alone!'

FOURTEEN

Dark *hated* being angry. The hot churning in his belly made him feel sick – and it hurt. For so many winters he'd buried all thoughts of his father. He felt as if someone had ripped off a scab and rubbed grit in the wound.

Or crystal, he thought sourly, chipping at the scarlet stone in his hand.

He had told Fin-Kedinn everything. In the gloom of false dawn they sat in the shelter, making arrows.

For the shafts, the Raven Leader had taken an alderwood shaft from one of his own arrows, and one made of sea buckthorn from a Whale Clan hunter. Dark was fashioning the arrowheads. The scarlet crystal was eerily easy to work: it wanted to take the shape of a birch leaf. Now almost finished, it lay on his knee on a wad of rawhide; he was pressure-flaking the edges with an antler tine.

Fin-Kedinn had already shortened his arrowshaft slightly to fit Renn, having measured her before she left, so that the finished arrow would be exactly her draw length plus half a thumb. Now he was making the shaft lighter, fining it down with a small beaver-tooth adze.

'If what Realvi told you about the Deep Forest is true,' he said without raising his eyes from his work, 'it's the best news we've had since the Thunderstar.'

Dark snorted. 'If we can believe him.'

'Odd that he didn't tell us sooner.'

'I asked him about that, but he weaselled out of it.'

'You don't trust him.'

'How can I?' Dark glowered at the crystal lying on his knee like a gout of blood. 'The day after my mother died he told me he was taking me into the Mountains to give me my clan-tattoos. Instead he left me. I was eight winters old. Why should I believe a word he says?'

Fin-Kedinn blew dust off the shaft. 'Is that arrowhead finished?'

Wordlessly, Dark handed it over.

He watched Fin-Kedinn scrape birch tar off the flat rock they'd placed by the fire, and daub some on the stem of the arrowhead. Expertly the Raven Leader slotted the stem into the tip of the shaft, then tied it in place with split reindeer tendon which he'd soaked in water. The tendon would shrink as it dried, binding the arrowhead even more securely.

The blue crystal lay forgotten in Dark's lap. It calmed him to watch Fin-Kedinn's strong, capable hands perform the tricky task of cutting a slot at the other end of the shaft, using sufficient force to make a groove that would take Renn's bowstring, without overdoing it and splitting the shaft.

Next Fin-Kedinn cut three flights from a partridge's reddish-brown tail-feather which he'd obtained from a Rowan Clan hunter. Having glued and bound each flight in place to make a neat, sure spiral, he trimmed them with a flint flake, skilfully removing any excess that would weigh down the arrow and lessen its speed, while leaving just enough feather to make it shoot true.

'Maybe your father really is sorry for what he did,' he said quietly.

Dark shook his head. 'I don't believe that. I can't trust him. That's all I know.' But what he found unbearable was that he *wanted* to trust Realvi. 'I wish you were my father,' he said.

Fin-Kedinn did not reply. Balancing the shaft on his forefinger, he scrutinized the finished arrow. Dark thought it was beautiful, perfect in its simplicity and usefulness.

'That's the first done,' Fin-Kedinn said briskly. 'Now for the blue arrow.' Beside him lay a heron feather supplied by Gaup's little girl, and some shredded seal gut provided by the Kelps.

'Don't you ever get tired of being Leader?' Dark burst out.

Fin-Kedinn surprised him by giving one of his rare chuckles. 'What would it matter if I did?'

'But surely—'

'Right now, Dark, everyone in camp is blaming everyone else for the Thunderstar. The Salmons and the Whales are blaming the rest of us because we mix things from the Forest with those of the Sea. The Rowans and Swans say we offend the fire every time we show it the soles of our boots. And on top of all that, someone's stealing from the food stores.' His blue eyes gleamed with humour. 'Now is not the time for me to get tired of being Leader.'

Dark envied him his strength and his calm. Unhappily he picked up the blue crystal, then put it down. 'I'll never find the ice crystal without Torak. He speaks wolf, I don't! My ankle's much better, you have to let me go and find him!'

To his dismay, Fin-Kedinn's face closed. 'You're the only Mage we have, Dark. Sunwake soon, we need you here.'

'But surely the Rite's more important even than Sunwake!'

'But how would you *find* Torak and Renn? You're still getting used to the Open Forest, you've never been near the Deep Forest—'

'You could tell me where to go!'

'Dark – no. We need you here.'

That night Dark learnt the answer to the mystery of the stolen food. He was returning from the midden when he caught movement at the corner of his eye: a shadow slipping behind a shelter. The shelter belonged to the Sea-eagles, who stored the camp's food in pits covered with stones. As the thief was sneaking away, Dark slipped round the other side and seized his hood.

Dark let go in disgust. 'You!'

Defiantly his father lifted his chin. He was clutching a wovenbark sack stuffed with frozen fish. 'What did you expect?' he sneered. 'When disaster strikes, it's every man for himself!'

'Not here,' said Dark.

'Yes, here! Time you grew up, Dark. Ask yourself this: where are your so-called friends now?'

'What do you mean?'

Realvi smirked. 'I just heard that they didn't go west on a scouting mission, they're headed for the Deep Forest! They didn't tell you that, did they? They slunk off in secret to save themselves!'

'How d'you find out where they went?'

'What's that matter? Point is, they left you behind!'

'That's not true, they left because—' He broke off. He'd caught a strange eager glint in his father's eyes: he was hanging on Dark's every word... A horrible suspicion began to take root. Could it be that his father was a spy? Was that why he and his companions had come to Crowwater? But who were they spying for?

'Give me that sack,' Dark said harshly. 'You might think it's every man for himself, but not here. Not with Fin-Kedinn as Leader.'

'Fin-Kedinn!' spat Realvi. 'You call him a Leader? You don't know what that means! In the Deep Forest we have a *real* Leader! He sees everything, knows everything! If he wanted to, he could grind Fin-Kedinn like a beetle under his heel!'

'I said give me that sack. Then get out of here.'

Moonlight glistened on Realvi's bony features. 'You're all cursed,' he hissed. 'Only we Chosen Ones will survive! The Great Leader protected us from the Thunderstar!'

'Who is this Great Leader of yours?'

The change in Realvi was startling, his face alight with fervour. 'He came out of the North, from the Edge of the World. He is beautiful as the sun, stronger than the strongest hunter! With a single sweep of his hand he will destroy this stinking camp as easily as a bear destroys a nest of wood-ants!'

He turned to run, but Dark grabbed his arm. With the speed of a snake Realvi spun round and kneed him in the groin. Dark crumpled in the snow.

'I'm not sorry I abandoned you in the Mountains,' spat Realvi. 'I'm sorry you *survived!* I should have strangled you at birth!'

'Get out of here before I strangle *you!*' gasped Dark.

Shouldering his sack, Realvi made to go – then turned

and bared his teeth in a grin. 'I almost forgot. That young wolf of yours… How do you know that he's safe?'

It was a ploy to get Dark out of the way, and by the time he realized this and had checked that Pebble and Darkfur were unharmed, his father was long gone, the other Swans with him.

Their tracks led east, but Fin-Kedinn gave orders to let them go. He said it was worth a sackful of fish to be rid of them.

'He's gone to tell his master,' Dark said bitterly when he and the Raven Leader were alone.

'This Leader of theirs,' said Fin-Kedinn. 'What makes you suspect it's the ice demon?'

'I don't suspect, I know! Everything Realvi told me fits with how Torak and Renn described him. Besides, I feel it here.' He struck his chest with his fist. 'There's a great evil in the Forest. Naiginn's alive. He rules the valleys south of the Shield, I'm sure of it!'

The Raven Leader did not reply. Dark sensed thoughts racing behind the unreadable features. 'And you think he sent Realvi and the others as spies,' Fin-Kedinn said at last.

'To find Torak and Renn, yes. Now you have to let me go! Soon Naiginn will know they survived the Thunderstar, he'll set the whole of the Deep Forest after them, he won't rest till they're dead! And they don't even know he's alive! Fin-Kedinn, you have let me find them!'

On the morning of Sunwake, Dark crested the ridge. Below him Crowwater Camp was still sunk in shadow. He thought of the hopeful people waiting to see the sun for the first time, to feel its healing warmth on their faces.

Turning east, he bowed, and spoke the charm of greeting to the crimson glow behind the Mountains. He watched Ark alight on a rock and shake out her feathers. She too was ready to welcome the sun.

Fin-Kedinn had given Dark his blessing: 'May the guardian fly with you.' More importantly, the Raven Leader had touched foreheads with him, almost as if Dark were his son.

Pebble came to stand beside him, panting and swinging his tail. The young wolf kept glancing back into the valley, and with a pang Dark realized why.

'You want to be with your mother,' Dark said sadly. 'I understand.' He sighed. He'd been hoping that Pebble would come with him to the Deep Forest, but this was not to be.

Pebble spat out a lump of ice he'd been chewing and rubbed his forehead affectionately against Dark's leg, making rar-rar noises and soft-biting his thigh.

Again Dark sighed. He wished he'd relented and let

Shamik come too. But someone had to look after Spike and the other creatures orphaned by the Thunderstar, and Shamik was only twelve summers old, it wouldn't be right to take her into danger.

Pebble was whining and nudging his thigh. His slanted eyes briefly met Dark's. He was saying farewell.

Dark stooped, and they touched noses. Then the young wolf trotted off down the slope, vanishing from sight within moments, a shadow melting into the dusky ruins of the Forest.

I always end up alone, thought Dark. Is it going to be like this my whole life?

Of course, he still had Ark, who, sensing his unhappiness, was staying especially close. But not even his beloved white raven could lessen the loneliness, the anger and the shame. His father was a thief and a spy, intent on betraying Torak and Renn to his master...

The sun was rising. As Dark stood up to go, something glinted at his feet. He blinked.

The answer lies in the jaws of the wolf...

It was the lump of ice which Pebble had spat out.

Except it wasn't ice. It was crystal. A ray of pure, clear light turned to stone.

FIFTEEN

'I told you,' gasped Torak. 'I come as a friend!'

His captor struck him a dizzying blow to the temple. '*Friends* leave footprints, enemies hide their tracks!'

'*Friends*,' said another with a kick in the guts, 'don't disguise themselves as one of us!'

'Or kill Honey-Eaters,' growled a third.

'I didn't kill that bear—'

A punch in the mouth, splitting his lip, spraying blood. 'How *dare* he name the Honey-Eater out loud!'

Seven Chosen Ones surrounded him, armed with axe, knife and spear. Aurochs: cruellest clan in the Deep Forest. Caked skulls, merciless eyes in chalk-white faces ridged with scars.

With brutal efficiency they'd pinioned his arms behind his back and stripped him of his gear, ripping the wrist-guard from his forearm, the slate wolf from his neck, taking his medicine pouch and the spare knife tied to his calf. In outrage at his disguise they'd scrubbed off every speck of chalk with clumps of frozen thistles till his skin was raw. Silently he prayed they wouldn't catch Renn.

'Surely one of you recognizes me?' he protested, struggling to his knees. 'I was here three summers ago! I'm half Deep Forest myself, my mother was Red Deer, take a look at my medicine horn!'

'An unbeliever lie!' cried the man who'd split his lip. He had a broken nose like a squashed mushroom, and from the look in his eyes he was enjoying having a prisoner at his mercy.

'*And* he killed the Furred One!' Another man indicated the bear's mutilated carcass.

'I didn't touch it! Can't you see that bear's frozen stiff? It's been dead for days!'

'It's forbidden to name the Furred One!' Shaking with rage, the man thrust his face at Torak's. His eyes were bloodshot, his chalk-stiffened beard moulded in spikes like icicles.

'What's that mark on his forehead?' said the man with the broken nose. Grabbing Torak by the hair, he wrenched back his head and peered at his brow — then flung him down with a cry.

Ice Beard also drew back, as did the others, their chalky fingers seeking the auroch-horn amulets on their parkas. They were frightened. Torak could smell it.

'It has the mark!' whispered Broken Nose. 'A quartered circle tattooed on the brow, just as the Leader foresaw!' With the tip of his spear he pushed down the neck of Torak's parka.

More gasps of alarm.

'A ragged scar on the breastbone,' breathed Ice Beard. 'Again, just as the Leader said!'

Broken Nose was nodding. 'It bears the marks of the Skin-Taker.'

Torak was aghast. 'But – I'm not a Skin-Taker!'

'Where's the other one?' demanded Broken Nose.

'I don't know what you mean,' lied Torak.

'The female Skin-Taker! Where is she?'

'I don't know what you're talking about!'

Ice Beard spat in his face. 'Two Skin-Takers: that's what the Leader said we would find. He said the male would be a spirit walker, we'd know it by its marks, and the female would have red hair, she'd practise the foul rites of Magecraft!'

'I came *alone*,' insisted Torak. What in the name of the World Spirit was going on?

The Chosen Ones were now too frightened to go on beating him up. As they stuffed his gear in a wovenbark sack, they took care not to touch it with their bare hands. Nor would they look at him when they slung a horsehair noose round his neck and began dragging him towards the Windriver.

'I am not a Skin-Taker,' he repeated. 'Why would a Skin-Taker carry a medicine horn full of earthblood?'

'Skin-Takers are full of tricks,' muttered Broken Nose. 'Our Leader warned us not to believe anything they say.'

Snow pattering onto his head made Torak glance up. Rip was perched on a branch, peering down at him. Silently Torak begged the raven to protect Renn. Rip hitched his wings and flew away. Torak didn't think the Chosen Ones had noticed.

Ice Beard was shaking his head, trying to take it in. 'The Leader foresaw *every detail* of those marks,' he said with reverence.

In a flash it came to Torak: he knew who their Leader was. 'Your Leader foresaw my scar and my tattoo,' he told them, 'because he's seen me before.'

A spear jabbed between his shoulder blades. "Course he has!' retorted Broken Nose. 'He roams the Forest, protecting us from evil!'

'No, he saw me in the Far North,' countered Torak. 'He's Narwal Clan, his name's Naiginn.'

Broken Nose gave a derisive bark. 'D'you think we don't know that? As a boy the Leader was fostered with us – but Naiginn was only his *mortal* name!'

'The moon before the Thunderstar struck,' said Ice Beard, 'he returned to us from the Far North. He was Naiginn no longer. He'd changed: his mortal flesh burnt away to reveal his true power!'

'And he used it at once,' another put in breathlessly.

'There had been sickness in our clan: sickness which our old Leader couldn't cure. Then the Sacred One told us why: *it was because our old Leader was himself a Skin-Taker!*'

'The Sacred One alone can detect a Skin-Taker at a glance,' said Broken Nose. 'After he killed the old Leader he became our ruler, our protector!'

'And I suppose,' Torak couldn't help adding, 'all the sick people suddenly got better.' The Narwal Clan used poison when hunting; doubtless Naiginn had caused the sickness himself, then swiftly 'cured' it by withholding the poison.

But the Chosen Ones weren't listening. 'We owe our lives to the Leader,' one said fervently.

'He fought off the Thunderstar—'

'—and now he guards the Forest, protecting us from Skin-Takers.'

'When they come in the night he transforms himself into a Furred One to hunt them—'

'You mean he turns into a bear?' exclaimed Torak. Another jab reminded him not to name the creature out loud.

'As a Furred One,' intoned Broken Nose, 'our Leader prowls the Forest, keeping us safe.'

Torak realized that talking to them was futile. They were utterly in thrall to Naiginn, they would obey his every command. And what Torak found truly terrifying was that they wouldn't listen to reason. No matter what proof he gave of his innocence, they would ignore him. Their minds were as rigid and shut as their white, scarred faces.

144

The trees were thinning. They had reached the frozen river. Three sleds stood waiting with teams of cowed and silent dogs. Broken Nose threw Torak onto a sled and lashed him to the struts, then took his place on the driver's step and cracked his whip.

Instantly the dogs set off at a run, their paws spattering Torak with ice. 'Where are you taking me?' he said over his shoulder.

'If I had my way,' said Broken Nose, 'I'd slit its throat and leave it for the crows. But then the Skin-Taker's foul spirit would go on doing evil.'

'We're taking it to the Leader,' called Ice Beard from his sled. 'Only the Leader knows how to kill a Skin-Taker in such a way that it stays dead!'

Wolf skittered to a halt, his paws slipping on the frozen Fast Wet.

He put up his muzzle to howl – then snapped it shut. Whining, he ran in circles. The White Taillesses had taken his pack-brother on the sliding trees, and more White Taillesses were hunting the pack-sister. She had watched her mate captured and was now toiling after him, moving slowly and keeping to the cover of the trees as she floundered through drifts.

Wolf couldn't protect them both. Which one should he help?

The ravens who belonged to the pack swooped low, wingbeats ruffling his fur. For a tail-flick his glance met theirs, then shifted to the pack-sister. They understood and veered after her.

Wolf felt a bit better. The pack-sister was wily, she knew how to hide, and the ravens would look after her. He raced off in pursuit of his pack-brother.

The dogs' scent trail was so thick that a newborn cub could have followed it, and their speed no match for Wolf's. Soon he was loping alongside, effortlessly keeping pace while remaining unseen and unsmelt among the pines.

Tall Tailless was huddled on one of the sliding trees. Wolf felt a growl scratch his gullet as he scented his pack-brother's blood; Tall Tailless's muzzle was dark with it.

Sensing Wolf's presence, Tall Tailless turned his head and fiercely met his gaze: *Stay away!*

Wolf was startled. Beneath his pack-brother's pain and fear was a blazing urge to fight. This made no sense. No wolf would think about fighting when he was in the middle of a stranger pack, he would do everything he could to escape.

But although Wolf's pack-brother had the heart and spirit of a wolf, he was a tailless – and taillesses are not the same as wolves. They can keep their anger alive and snarling inside them for many Lights and Darks, which is a thing no real wolf ever does. Until now, Wolf had not sensed such ferocity in his pack-brother. It worried him.

The Up was darkening, shadows creeping between the pines, and still Wolf kept pace with the dogs pulling the sliding trees. A herd of reindeer raised their heads to watch him pass. An otter saw him coming and bounded away.

Again wings swished overhead. Wolf glanced up, and nearly crashed into a tree. The ravens – *his* ravens – were following Tall Tailless, and that meant the pack-sister was alone and unprotected.

What should Wolf do now?

SIXTEEN

The sled tracks shouted at Renn from the frozen river.

If she left the cover of the alders on the bank and dropped onto the ice, she could go much faster – but she would stand out like a raven on an ice floe. And for all she knew, the Forest might be crawling with Skin-Takers and Chosen Ones.

With a sigh she trudged in her snowshoes up the elk trail that followed the bank. Its compacted hoof-prints made walking less arduous, and the elk had cleverly kept to dense thickets and hidden hollows.

Renn had sent the ravens after Torak, begging them to help him – but she missed them now. In her mind she saw him, bloodied and bruised but grimly defiant as his captors flung him onto the sled. Snatches of overheard speech had confirmed her worst fears: Naiginn was alive, and he'd tricked the Deep Forest clans into making him Leader. His mortal flesh burnt away to reveal his true power... A cunning way of explaining the scars he'd acquired in the Far North.

Torak had demanded to know where they were taking him, but the Chosen Ones' answer had been lost in the crack of whips and the scrape of runners. All Renn knew was that they'd headed east up the frozen river. The stone in her stomach told her they were taking him to Naiginn: that her nightmare was about to come true.

Every detail was incised in her memory. Torak trapped in ice, his neck bared to Naiginn's knife. Naiginn crouching beside him, slurping the brains of the newborn seal. *Brains taste of souls, but I want the souls themselves. And for that I need to eat them alive...*

An owl called to its mate. From across the river came the long, echoing reply.

Don't think about Naiginn, Renn told herself firmly. Don't think about how slowly you're going, or how hopeless it is to be following dog sleds on foot...

Dusk came on and a light snow fell, spindrift flowing around her boots. The Forest was hushed except for a distant clamour of crows gathering to roost. The first night of the moon's dark, but Renn had no intention of pitching camp. She would track the sleds by snowglow.

She started at every groaning trunk, picturing Chosen Ones slipping between the pines. Every tree-shadow became a tall thin hunter.

Wolf had raced after Torak, but part of her wished he'd stayed at her side. Wolf could see in the dark. His nose was so keen he could scent Chosen Ones long before they appeared.

As night deepened, she realized she'd lost her bearings. The Shield, for so long a towering presence to the north, had dwindled to a low spur, finally swallowed by the Forest.

A wren's deafening alarm call made her jump. The tiny furious bird was bobbing up and down in a hazel bush: *Cha-cha-cha! This is my bush! Go away!*

Its calls continued long after Renn had left it behind.

Her belly rumbled. She was so hungry she could eat a lemming. Only that morning she and Torak had finished their supplies. It felt like a moon ago.

Through the trees she caught the steady sound of chomping. The boar was as big as a canoe, rooting around with its snout for leftover acorns. Boars have the keenest noses next to wolves, and this one had smelt Renn long before she'd seen it. It eyed her as she passed, but went on chomping.

The snow ceased. Smoke-frost floated above the river, faintly aglow in the starlight. On the opposite bank Renn made out a herd of bison, hazed with spangled breath. Slowly, purposefully, they made their way onto the ice and started ambling upstream.

She came to a log where a squirrel had eaten its nightmeal, leaving a litter of beechnut casings and acorn cups. She was out of luck: the squirrel hadn't left a single nut.

On one side of the log she found the small black squidgy mushrooms the clans call 'demon droppings'. They were said to taste like slugs, but Renn wasn't desperate enough to try them. Spotting a horsehoof mushroom on a trunk, she cut it into chunks. It was as tough and tasteless as rawhide, but filled her up.

From the river came a low rumbling: the bisons were moving closer. She found herself gazing down at shaggy mountains of muscle, bearded heads crowned by crescent-moon horns.

Like the boar, the bison knew they had nothing to fear from her. She found their huffing breath and musky smell reassuring. They were telling her: *Keep going, we are here.*

In the distance a wolverine bounded onto the ice and rose on its hind legs to survey the herd. Wolverines are fearless, and attack prey ten times their size. This one decided the herd was too strong, and bounded off into the dark.

Ahead the river forked around an island of spindly birches glittering with frost. The bison herd split too, flowing like a dark flood up both frozen streams.

For all their bulk, they moved faster than Renn. She was sorry when she could no longer see them or hear their rumbling breath.

It was only when she drew level with the island that she realized they'd obliterated the tracks of the Chosen Ones' sleds.

In disbelief she jumped down onto the river. All she found was trampled ice, spattered with faintly steaming dung.

A sob rose in her throat. She had no way of knowing which fork the Chosen Ones had taken.

As she climbed back onto the bank, she startled woodpigeons which exploded from the undergrowth with a clap of wings. Whipping an arrow from her quiver, she fired. A pigeon dropped like a stone. Her triumph was short-lived. The carcass had snagged high in a spruce.

The spruce seemed friendlier than most Deep Forest trees, extending sturdy branches for Renn to climb. Having tied her snowshoes to her pack, she shinned up its trunk like a squirrel.

She was so hungry she stayed where she was in the branches and ate the pigeon raw: the warm, sweet, slippery liver, the tough little heart, the deliciously chewy flesh. After leaving an offering of feathers, she stuffed what was left in her pack, to deal with later.

With hunger gone, the stark truth came crashing back. She had no idea where the Chosen Ones had taken Torak.

Not far off, another wren was sounding the alarm.

Renn stiffened.

Twenty paces away through the trees, she made out the thin grey figures of yet another band of Chosen Ones.

Silently they wove towards her, ashen heads turning from side to side, chalky fingers flickering in wordless speech. Soundlessly they passed beneath her – and on into the shadows. Moments later she saw them dropping from the riverbank onto the ice.

She breathed out.

It occurred to her that if she followed them, they would very likely lead her to Torak. But even if she managed to stay hidden, they probably had dog sleds waiting somewhere ahead, so once again she'd be left behind.

For an instant she despaired. Was there no other way?

Then it came to her. Only one thing to do.

Scrambling down from the spruce, she went after them.

She hadn't put on her snowshoes, and floundered knee-deep until she found the Chosen Ones' tracks and ran in them.

She left the trees and stepped out onto the bank. She called after them in a loud clear voice: 'Here I am!'

SEVENTEEN

It didn't take Renn long to realize that she'd made a terrible mistake. Not only had Naiginn tricked the Chosen Ones into making him Leader, he'd duped them into believing she was a Skin-Taker.

'But if I was a Skin-Taker,' she protested as they were binding her hands, 'why would I call out to you?'

'Don't listen to it, it's a trick!' spat a scrawny Forest Horse hunter with a white, weasely face.

Renn appealed to the Bat Clan hunter who seemed to be in charge. 'How can shouting, "Here I am," be a trick?'

He was older than the others and built like a bison, with short legs and massive shoulders. His head and beard were stiff with pitch, and from under the heavy ledge of

154

his brows peered a pair of shrewd dark eyes. 'If you're not a Skin-Taker,' he growled, 'what are you doing here?'

'The Forest north of the Shield was destroyed,' she replied. 'Survivors are camped at Crowwater Caves. Fin-Kedinn – he's Leader of the Raven Clan—'

'I know who he is,' he cut in.

'He's my bone kin, he sent me to find out if there's any Forest left alive!'

'You'd have seen that from the Shield. Why come so far in?'

She hesitated. 'Fin-Kedinn gave me a message for your Leader,' she lied, unwilling to mention the Rite.

'What message?' he said suspiciously.

'I'm to tell only your Leader.'

'I don't believe you. If you meant no harm, why sneak past our borders, why not declare yourself openly?'

'I just did!'

'How did you know which way to come?'

'We didn't—'

'Who's we?' he said sharply.

No point lying about Torak. If they didn't yet know he'd been taken captive, they soon would. 'He's my mate,' she said. 'The Aurochs caught him, they—'

'The *Chosen Ones*,' corrected the Forest Horse hunter. 'We're one clan now!' His eyes were bloodshot and he kept clenching and unclenching his fists. Renn could see the violence working in him and in the others: two Forest Horses and three Bat Clan, all much younger than the man in charge. They looked as if they'd like nothing better than to prove themselves men by beating up a girl.

She turned to the big man. 'We're wasting time. I have to get to your camp and deliver my message!'

He bristled. 'You're in no position to tell me what to do.'

The weaselly one shifted impatiently. 'Why talk to it, Iakim? Every word it spits out is a lie!'

Renn ignored him. 'You've seen my belt, my medicine pouch and my horn,' she told the man called Iakim. 'Can't you see I'm a Mage, not a Skin-Taker?'

To her alarm this provoked roars of outrage from the others. The weaselly one slapped her, knocking her backwards onto the ice. 'Out of its own mouth it condemns itself!' he shrieked. 'Magecraft is *forbidden!*'

Again he raised his fist, but Iakim yanked him back. 'That's enough, Tseid! We don't hit women.'

'This is no woman, it's a Skin-Taker!'

'While I'm in command, you'll do as I say! And that goes for the rest of you!' Dispassionately he watched Renn struggle to her feet. 'Some of what she says could be true. She looks like Fin-Kedinn's kin, I saw her three summers ago.'

'This creature merely *resembles* her!' cried a Bat Clan boy. 'Skin-Takers can take any form they like.'

'That's true too,' conceded Iakim. 'Only the Leader will know for sure.'

Tseid contented himself with a snarl, but when Iakim's back was turned he thrust his face in Renn's. The chalk on his skin was cracked and his breath was rank. 'My sister was a Skin-Taker,' he hissed. 'We never knew it till the Leader saw the birthmark on her neck. I was glad they killed her. She'd dishonoured our kin!'

'That's enough,' snapped Iakim. 'We need to get going.'

They started trudging upriver with Renn in their midst, her bruised cheek throbbing, thoughts darting like ants.

It was a frosty night, echoing with the cries of owls fighting for territory. To Renn's dismay she could see no dog sleds waiting on the ice. Did her captors intend to walk to their camp? Meanwhile the Aurochs might already have reached it, they might be dragging Torak before Naiginn...

She stumbled, would have fallen if Iakim hadn't hauled her upright. 'Thanks,' she muttered.

He grunted.

'Do you really shun Magecraft?' she said quietly.

His heavy brows sank in a scowl. 'Mages say they can see the future, but that's a lie. They didn't foresee the Thunderstar.'

'And your Leader did?'

'Better than that, he protected us from it.'

'Was he the one who forbade Magecraft?'

He shot her an angry glance. 'Our Leader speaks for the World Spirit. He's right to shun the old ways. If we don't, the Thunderstar might strike again.'

Looking up at his harsh, thoughtful face, she wondered if he truly believed that.

'He is more powerful than any Mage,' he went on, as if talking to himself. 'I've seen him bring a dead Honey-Eater back to life...'

Renn was silent. She guessed that Naiginn had simply drugged a live bear, then waited for the poison to wear off. But she would only antagonize Iakim if she tried to discredit 'the Leader'.

Ahead of them the others were sneering at her gear. Tseid brandished her bow, sniffed it, made a face. 'Salmon Clan! Reeks of the Sea! If that's not proof of evil I don't know what is!' Snapping the bow in two, he flung it across the ice.

Renn stifled a cry. 'He shouldn't have done that,' she said under her breath.

Iakim heard: he must have the ears of a bat. 'Wasn't much of a bow,' he remarked.

'But a bow just the same,' she said hotly. 'It didn't deserve to be treated like that!'

Something gleamed in his deepset eyes. A flash of understanding?

Two owls sped shrieking across the river and crashed into a snowdrift, lashing out at each other with beak and claw. The fight didn't last long, the victor flying off into the pines, leaving a wreck of bloody feathers in the snow.

'That's the third time I've seen owls fight to the death,' murmured Iakim. 'Stranger things too – murdered trees, a Honey-Eater's mutilated carcass...' Raising his head, he scanned the stars. 'Chaos and disorder... The Deep Forest survived the Thunderstar, but without the First Tree it's doomed. And there's nothing we can do.'

'I don't believe that,' said Renn. For a moment she was tempted to tell him about the Rite. 'That man called Tseid,' she added. 'He has a sickness in his eyes, that's why they're red. There's raspberry root in my medicine pouch, and blackberry leaves—'

Iakim turned on her. 'Magecraft is *forbidden*! If he's sick it's the will of the World Spirit, it'd be wrong to intervene!'

'Do you believe that?'

He drew himself up. 'I see what you're trying to do,' he said coldly. 'You want to gain my trust. The Leader was right. It's nothing but a Skin-Taker trick!'

EIGHTEEN

The dog sleds swept into the camp of the Chosen Ones and strong hands flung Torak into a dazzle of torchlight.

They had travelled all day and into the night. From what he'd overheard they had reached the place where two rivers flowed down from the Mountains and became the Windriver.

As his eyes adjusted to the glare, he made out a huddle of snow-covered shelters. The Chosen Ones were camped on the frozen river itself.

The man he thought of as Ice Beard – Torak still didn't know his name – untied his ankles and hauled him to his feet. Cramped from confinement, his legs gave way. Again

Ice Beard hauled him upright. 'Get moving,' he growled, giving him a shove in the back.

A silent throng of men, women and children parted to let them through. Chalked faces regarded him with as little feeling as hunters preparing to butcher a carcass.

Blood crackled in Torak's nostrils and crusted his mouth. He spat. 'Where's your Leader?' he rasped.

For all the answer he got, he might have spoken to the moon.

The shelters were left behind. He smelt stale blood and found himself craning his neck at an enormous frozen waterfall. Where the two rivers crashed together and thundered over a cliff, the torrent had been stilled by a touch of the World Spirit's finger. Above him towered a silent tumult: icicles longer than trees, waiting till next spring to fall. They gleamed blue in the starlight, except for a great dark stain spilling from halfway up, where firelight glimmered redly in a cave.

Beneath the cave two huge pine trunks, notched with footholds, had been propped against the ice. These ladders were heavily guarded. Torak thought he recognized three of the Swans who'd been at Crowwater, including Dark's father, Realvi. In an instant Torak understood how Naiginn had known that he and Renn had survived the Thunderstar.

Winged shadows cut across the stars, and he glimpsed Rip and Rek circling noiselessly. From time to time on the journey he'd spotted the ravens keeping pace with the sleds. He didn't know if this was good or bad. Did it mean they were trying to help him, or had the Chosen Ones also caught Renn?

Nobody else heeded the ravens, all eyes were fixed on the cave. Its red glow intensified, and from it burst a bear's heart-stopping roar.

With one voice the crowd cried out. As one being, people sank to their knees.

A shadow loomed against the cavelight. Torak glimpsed heavy fur robes, a long pale mane rigid with chalk, a glaring white face crowned with a spiny circlet of bear claws. Naiginn had found a cunning way of concealing the burns he'd sustained in the Far North – and on the pretext of uniting his followers as a single clan, he had insisted that they all do the same.

Broken Nose grabbed Torak's hair and yanked back his head. In a reverent voice he called to his Leader: 'Great One, we bring you a Skin-Taker!'

Cries of horror rang out from the crowd. Mothers pulled children close. Men brandished weapons at Torak.

The voice that issued from the cave dispelled any lingering doubts that this was Naiginn. Smooth, strong, made to instil trust and sway a mob, it raised the hairs on the back of Torak's neck. 'What, this scrap of a boy?' it sneered. 'A Skin-Taker? Are you *sure*?'

'It has the marks, as you foretold!' called Ice Beard.

'If that isn't proof enough,' cried Broken Nose, 'we caught it beside the carcass of a murdered Honey-Eater!'

Groans of outrage from the crowd – instantly hushed as the shadowy figure raised its staff.

'Who would have thought such a feeble creature could conceal so much evil?' Naiginn spoke calmly, with sorrowful wisdom. 'Now do you see, my children, that there's no end to the lies and tricks of the Skin-Takers?'

'We see, we see!' they moaned, abasing themselves in an ecstasy of obedience.

'And shall the Skin-Taker be slaughtered?'

'Kill it! Kill it!' they roared, closing in with spears, axes, knives.

The mask-like face remained inscrutable, but its eyes sought Torak's. *I'm enjoying this. Are you?*

Torak's thoughts were racing. At a word from Naiginn, they would cut him to pieces. Why then was he still alive? Did Naiginn want to do the killing himself, to avenge the injuries he'd suffered in the Far North?

There had to be more to it than that. Naiginn was an ice demon trapped in the body of a man: above all he wanted to be free, to wreak havoc on living creatures. To gain his freedom he must break the spell that bound his demon souls – and for that he needed Renn.

He hasn't got her! thought Torak with a surge of hope. That's why he's keeping me alive. He thinks he can use me as bait to catch her...

Suddenly two things happened at once.

The ravens swept low over the people, making them duck, then perched cawing on the ladders. At the same moment Wolf's howls echoed through the night: *I'm coming! Where — are — you?*

Torak flung up his head and howled a response: *Too dangerous! Stay away!*

Wolf's puzzled reply: *I hear you, pack-brother!*

The crowd faltered and drew back.

Torak glared at them. 'Could a Skin-Taker talk to wolves?' he shouted. 'Would a wolf, the wisest hunter in the Forest, answer a Skin-Taker?'

'Don't be fooled, my children,' warned Naiginn from his cave. 'A Skin-Taker when it's cornered tries any trick it can! Those marks don't lie! *This* is the evil one which haunts your nights and poisons your dreams! Which cuts the Death Marks from the flesh of your loved ones, so that it may feed!'

The mob forgot about Wolf. Again it closed in.

Again Naiginn's power restrained them. 'None may touch it!' he commanded. 'If any of you tried to kill it, it would shrivel your souls and scatter them shrieking for ever! Only the Great Leader has the skill to root the evil from the Skin-Taker's marrow, to grind it to dust! Bring the Skin-Taker to my cave!'

Torak's captors dragged him towards the ladder. As Rip glided away, the raven caught Torak's eye and glanced down at the snow.

In the uncertain torchlight Torak saw that Rip had dropped a flint flake at the foot of the nearest ladder. Torak had a heartbeat to act. Pretending to stumble, he fell face down, grabbed the flake between his lips.

'No tricks!' muttered Ice Beard, dragging him to his feet.

'I slipped,' Torak replied. The flint was small enough to stow in his cheek without affecting his speech. He had no idea how he might use it, but the feel of it gave him hope.

They were tying a rope to his wrists behind him, hauling him up one of the ladders. Agonizing pain in his shoulders as his arms were wrenched back and up, his feet scrabbling in vain for footholds.

Just when he thought his joints would crack, he was hoisted over the top and into the cave. Now the Chosen Ones were tying his wrists to his ankles, then bowing themselves out and disappearing down the ladders.

Silence after they'd gone. A smoky glimmer of torchlight, the rank smell of bear fat. Beneath it the charnel stink of death.

Torak struggled to his knees, his bonds forcing him to lean awkwardly backwards. A blow to the head knocked him sideways.

Spots swam before his eyes. A club loomed into view, studded with bear teeth. A white mask bent over him. With deliberate care the club was laid aside, and a knife held close to his face. It was of glossy black flint, gripped in a fist clad in a bearskin gauntlet tufted with fur. From each fingertip jutted a long, lethal claw.

Slowly, the knife stroked Torak's cheek. Warmth trickled down his neck. The black flint was so sharp that all he felt was the heat of his blood – until Naiginn rubbed ash in the wound.

'To make sure it scars,' he said calmly.

'Why bother?' gasped Torak. 'I won't live long enough to heal.'

The chalked features cracked in a smile. 'Maybe you will. I'm going to scar you as you scarred me. And I'm going to do the same to Renn.'

He's lying, Torak told himself. He hasn't got her. That's why he's keeping me alive.

'It's no lie,' said Naiginn as if he'd heard. 'I've got her all right. But I know your tricks, I'm not stupid enough to have her brought to the same camp.'

'If you've got her, what d'you want with me?'

The rank smell of bear intensified as Naiginn leant closer. 'Every soul I eat makes me stronger,' he murmured. 'And I want yours more than most—'

'Because I'm a spirit walker: something you'll never be!'

Naiginn flinched. 'After I've scarred you,' he said coldly, 'I'm going to cut open your skull. Then your power will be mine.' Bending nearer, he whispered: 'I'm going to eat your brains!'

NINETEEN

Wolf crept unsmelt towards the great Den of the White Taillesses. They were asleep. So were their dogs, small slumbering mounds in the Bright Soft Cold that was steadily falling.

Sneaking past on silent paws, Wolf followed his pack-brother's scent over the frozen Fast Wet. He reached the bottom of the tall fanged cliffs of Bright Hard Cold.

Amid all the smells he caught the strange scent he'd encountered at the bear carcass: the scent of demon and bear, chewed up together. Beneath that, a whiff of his pack-brother. Wolf smelt pain, fear, loneliness. Did Tall Tailless think Wolf had abandoned him?

Now Wolf heard taillesses somewhere above. It was

coming from a cave halfway up the fanged cliff. Wolf heard his pack-brother gasping – and the yip-and-yowl of another tailless: very strong and very cruel.

Wolf's hackles bristled, and in his chest a growl fought to get out. Taillesses are good at changing their overpelts and hiding their scents, but they can't alter their voices. Wolf knew at once that the tailless in that cave was none other than the demon from the treeless lands: the demon who had captured the pack-sister and shot Wolf in the rump, the demon who had tried to kill his pack-brother.

With a snarl Wolf leapt at the Bright Hard Cold. He fell back, leapt again. No matter how often he sprang, clawed, scrabbled, the fanged cliffs flung him off. Wolf ran this way and that, seeking another way up. The rocks on either side were too steep, he couldn't do it.

It crashed upon him that he'd made a terrible mistake. He should have listened to Tall Tailless when he'd howled at him to stay away. On his own, Wolf was as helpless to save his pack-brother as a newborn cub.

The dogs were waking: shaking the Bright Soft Cold from their fur, straining at their tethers, making strange wheezy yowls, as if they wanted to bark but couldn't.

White Taillesses were crawling out their Dens. They saw Wolf. Their muzzles fell open.

Wolf sped off into the Forest. He knew now that he couldn't rescue Tall Tailless on his own.

He had to find the pack-sister.

'What's happening?' cried Renn. 'Why are we turning round?'

'I heard a shout,' said Iakim. With a flick of his whip he'd brought his dogs about, turning the sled back the way they'd come and heading to the others, who were still out of sight behind a bend.

Renn had lost track of how long they'd been racing up the frozen river. Her mind shied away from what Naiginn might be doing to Torak in the meantime.

'Why the impatience?' Iakim said drily. 'Are you so desperate to deliver that so-called "message" to our Leader?' His tone told her plainly that he knew the message didn't exist.

'I don't care about reaching camp,' she lied.

'Not even if they kill your mate?'

'Not even then.' She hated saying it, but her only hope of rescuing Torak was to feign indifference, while finding some way of persuading Iakim to let her go before they reached camp.

Tied to the cross-struts, she lay racking her brains.

Then she saw why Iakim had turned back. One of the other sleds had broken through a patch of thin ice. Its rear end was sinking, the front end tilting skywards, the dogs frantically straining, uttering the muffled whines that were the only sounds they seemed capable of making. The ice was smooth as slate, the sled dragging them towards an ever-widening maw of murky water. The others had halted their sleds and were trying to pull the dogs clear. Tseid, lying on his side to spread his weight, was sliding towards the stricken sled to grab it.

Slewing to a halt, Iakim ran to help. He was twice as strong as the others, and with his aid they soon hauled both dogs and sled out of danger.

But to Renn's horror, instead of heading off again, the big man declared a halt to rest the dogs, and everyone made for the bank. Iakim woke a fire while Tseid and the others yanked their wet parkas over their heads and blotted them dry in the snow.

Still tied to the sled, Renn ground her teeth. The men huddled round the flames, taking strips of dried meat from food pouches and silently gnawing. Tseid darted angry glances at her, clearly blaming the captive Skin-Taker for the accident.

Iakim came and hunkered down to check her bindings.

In desperation she asked if camp was much further.

'You can give up any hope of rescuing your mate,' he said through a mouthful of dried meat.

'I have,' she said.

The fire crackled, sparks flying upwards like souls in the night. Beyond the light the snow-covered Forest stood silent.

Feeling eyes on her, Renn turned her head.

Wolf was almost invisible among the pines, his eyes shining redly in the firelight. For a moment they locked gazes. Then Wolf's eyes blinked out and he was gone.

Never had Renn wished more fervently that she understood wolf talk. Earlier she'd heard him howling. Moments later she'd caught Torak's distant reply. What had they been saying? What had Wolf tried to tell her just now?

Iakim was still on his haunches, tightening the straps that bound her. 'Strange,' he muttered. 'For days there's been talk of a great grey wolf that comes and goes as silently as snow.' He paused. 'Just now I saw it looking at you. Can you speak to it?'

'Him,' she murmured. 'Wolf is a him.'

Sinking his chin inside his parka so that the others wouldn't see him talking, he said: 'I've been asking myself whether a Skin-Taker would offer to heal a Chosen One's eyes. Whether a Skin-Taker would care if her bow were snapped in two. Unless…'

Renn also lowered her chin so that the others couldn't see. 'Unless?' she prompted.

'Unless these are more tricks to gain my trust.'

She sucked in her breath. 'What do you think?'

'I don't know.' He hesitated. 'Something else. A few days before the Thunderstar struck, my mother's sister died of the falling sickness. We put her body in her Death Tree, a long way back west. Later – after the Thunderstar – I returned to make an offering for her souls.' His eyes met hers. 'Skin-Takers had sliced off her Death Marks. They'd taken her tongue, her eyes… But something didn't fit.'

His voice sank to a whisper. 'Someone had given her *new* Death Marks – and that someone had left tracks.

171

Their boots were of a kind we don't make in the Deep Forest, coils of dogfish sewn to their soles to improve the grip.' He glanced at the soles of Renn's boots. 'I've been asking myself why a Skin-Taker would give a body new Death Marks.'

'Because I'm not a Skin-Taker and you know it!' she said urgently. 'I'm a Mage! I'm here to do a Rite.' Briefly, she told him about the four arrows. '*That's* why I'm so impatient! I don't care about reaching camp, I don't have a message for your Leader – and I don't care about my mate!' (Forgive me, Torak.) 'The only thing that matters is the Rite – and time's short, I have to do it by the third night of the moon's dark. Now do you see why you *have* to let me go? It's the only chance we have of bringing back the First Tree!'

The Bat Clan hunter was listening intently, his expression giving nothing away. 'This Rite – *if* you haven't made it up. Where would you do it?'

'There are places in the Forest which you can only find when you're lost. That's all I know.'

He snorted. 'Now I know you're a Mage! Never a straight answer!'

'So will you help me?'

His scowl deepened. 'Tell me. Did you foresee the Thunderstar?'

'No,' she admitted. 'Last autumn I saw signs that something terrible was coming, but I didn't know what. None of us did.'

'Can you wonder that we've turned against Magecraft?'

172

'But you still care about the Forest! If there's even the smallest chance that this Rite will work, surely—'

'Enough! You lied to me before and you're lying now!'

Before she could speak he'd stomped back to the others. She couldn't hear what he was telling them but they sprang up, some flinging snow on the fire to put it back to sleep, others gathering gear and hurrying to rejoin their sleds.

Tseid was remonstrating with the big man. 'First you want to rest the dogs, now you want to press on!'

Whatever Iakim's reply, the smaller man judged it best to obey, and within moments whips were cracking and the dogs were setting off at a run, this time with Tseid and the other sleds taking the lead, and Iakim and Renn in the rear.

Once again she was jolting over the ice, no hope of escape. The pines on the bank watched her go. The frosty stars were indifferent to her fate. She had failed. Soon she would be brought to the camp of the Chosen Ones and Naiginn would kill her – as he had doubtless already killed Torak.

The next moment she knew she was wrong. If Torak was dead, Wolf would have been devastated. Instead he'd been urgent and intent... Could that mean he'd found Torak? Was that what he'd been trying to tell her?

Iakim swerved to avoid another patch of new ice. Ahead of them the others had disappeared round another bend.

Abruptly, Iakim halted. Before Renn knew what was happening, he'd whipped out his axe and was hacking a hole in the new ice. Now he was cutting her free. 'Go,' he muttered. 'Before I change my mind!'

When she didn't move he picked her up and carried her to the bank, tossed her in the snow. 'I'll tell them you tried to escape and fell through the ice. Here...' Thrusting her axe and her medicine pouch into her hands, he pulled her to her feet and gave her a push.

'Do the Rite! Bring back the First Tree! Go!'

For the twitch of a tail Wolf had lost the pack-sister – he'd thought she was still on the sliding tree – but it hadn't taken long to realize that she'd escaped. *Clever* pack-sister!

He found her by her howl: wobbly as a cub's, but full of feeling. They wasted little time in greetings, just a swift nose-rub. The demon had Tall Tailless: Wolf *had* to make her follow.

But to his astonishment she wouldn't.

Wolf grunt-barked and bounded up the trail, raced back, telling her with every twitch of his ears and lash of his tail that she *had to follow*. She ignored him – although he sensed that she was just as desperate to find Tall Tailless.

But what was she *doing*? She'd found a horse trail and was on her knees, fiddling with a chunk of tree-root she'd hacked from a stump. Now she was unwinding a length of deer tendon from around her leg and tying it to the root.

The horse trail was littered with fresh dung, Wolf couldn't resist rolling in it to hide his scent. He rubbed against the pack-sister, she batted him away.

Suddenly he heard horses moving towards them. At first the pack-sister didn't, her little ears were too weak. Then she picked up the sound of swishing tails and crunching hooves.

Puzzled and frustrated, Wolf watched her hurriedly rubbing horse dung on the chunk of root and the looped tendon. Leaving them both carefully arranged on the trail, she darted behind a juniper bush, signing to Wolf with both forepaws to do the same.

Wolf's puzzlement turned to anger. What was she *doing*, hunting horses at a time like this, when Tall Tailless had been captured by the demon?

TWENTY

It's the Moon of the Salmon Run, and the Widewater is seething with fish. Its banks are foamy with meadow-sweet. Limes, alders and beeches are a vivid, throbbing green. The whole Forest is murmuring a welcome to the life-giving bounty swimming up from the Sea.

Standing in his canoe, Torak rakes his gaff along the river bottom. He snags a salmon, flicks it into the boat, where Dark ends its thrashing with his club. Torak wipes his forehead on his wrist and grins at his friend, then goes back to his work.

For as long as he can remember he's taken part in the salmon run. When he was little, he and Fa would labour for days on some out-of-the-way river. This spring, for the first time, Renn has persuaded him to fish with the Raven Clan. He'd grumbled – too many people – but now he's enjoying himself.

Everyone's happy, hard at work bringing in the catch. Men and boys are spearing the wriggling, gleaming fish, or setting willowbark nets across backwaters where the salmon pause to rest. Women and girls are deftly cutting off heads and tails and skewering them to dry; gutting, scraping silvery skins, slinging oily orange flesh on racks, packing deer stomachs with quivering mounds of roe, hanging them to smoke. Children are chopping logs for the fires, and sneaking into smoke-huts to filch delicious chewy fish eyes.

Everyone's taking turns guarding the racks, making sure the alderwood fires never sleep. Everyone's reeking of fish oil, and stuffed to the gullet with sweet succulent flesh and toasted hearts. And during the brief summer nights people tumble asleep, while the other Forest creatures continue to gorge. Bears, wolves, otters, lynx, wolverines, eagles, ravens, crows: many taking their catch into the Forest to eat in peace, their fishy leavings providing the trees with their share of the feast.

As Torak gaffs another salmon he hears Wolf howling his happiness to the Up. Darkfur and Pebble are in the shallows, teaching the cubs how to fish, and they—

The cubs? But the cubs are dead. They were killed by the Thunderstar.

Before Torak's eyes, the Forest withers and dies. Leaves shrivel, trees crash to earth.

He woke up. He was lying on his side, his elbows pinioned painfully behind his back, wrists tied to ankles. The charnel stink was sickening.

Dawn was breaking, chill blue daylight flooding the ice demon's lair. Through half-closed lids Torak made out the skull of an enormous bear mounted on a rock. Its eyes flickered red. He guessed a lamp had been set within. Beyond that, more daylight. Naiginn's cave had *two* mouths: one overlooking the Chosen Ones' camp, through which they'd dragged Torak the night before – and a second, on the other side of the frozen waterfall.

Torak was cramped and cold. His face was stiff with dried blood. The cut on his cheek hurt. Probing his mouth with his tongue, he found he still had the flake of flint. But what use was that?

A roar shook the cave. A giant shadow loomed.

Naiginn's bearskin robes were speckled with snow. He reeked of death. His clawed gauntlets were clogged with gobbets of yellow fat. His hair, dangling in rods of whitened clay, was streaked with dried blood.

Seeing that Torak was awake, his lip curled. 'So you came to at last,' he mocked. 'I should have known you'd faint as soon as I got started.'

'Why didn't you keep going?' croaked Torak.

'It's no fun if you can't feel it.' His ice-pale eyes had a filmy, sated look. Torak hated to think what he'd been eating. He'd been handsome once. Now his mask of cracked chalk only imperfectly concealed his scars. The burnt side of his face was puckered like wind-roughened ice. One ear had been scorched to a gristly nub.

Squatting beside Torak, he stroked his knife with a clawed forefinger, eyeing Torak's cheek, wondering where to make the next cut.

Torak saw the hunger for pain in the lightless black pupils. He forced himself to meet stare for stare. The ice demon knew no pity, no right or wrong. He fed on fear. The least sign of weakness and he'd strike like a snake.

He was vain too. Maybe by stoking his vanity, Torak could live a little longer...

Feigning calm, he said: 'Your people say you have the power to turn into a bear.'

The crusted lips parted to reveal teeth clogged with yellow grease. 'While they cower in their shelters, I prowl the Forest,' he jeered, 'bravely doing battle with the terrifying "Skin-Takers".'

Torak had a flash of insight. 'Who don't exist,' he said slowly.

Naiginn laughed. 'They exist because I say they do!'

Torak was silent. Naiginn ruled the Deep Forest through fear, feeding his people lies to keep them under his sway. 'You made up the whole thing,' he said. 'You're the one who slices off Death Marks and feeds on corpses.'

The pale eyes gleamed.

'But cutting off Death Marks...' mused Torak. 'That's not for show, you *have* to do it. You're a demon, you can't feed unless they're gone. That's why you wear those gauntlets: to protect you from earthblood.'

That pricked Naiginn's vanity. Torak had reminded him that there were limits to his power. 'I wear them because I like them,' he snapped. 'They come in useful when my prey is still alive.'

'Really?' taunted Torak. 'It's not that you're scared of earthblood?' He knew he was playing a lethally dangerous game, but he could see no other way. To Naiginn, control was everything: he needed Torak abject and cringing. He would keep him alive until he'd crushed his spirit.

'I'll show you something,' said Naiginn. Cutting the bond securing Torak's left ankle and wrist, he heaved him to the daylight at the other end of the cave, Torak hobbling awkwardly with his right wrist and ankle still tied together.

Below them stretched a desolate black waste. All the land between the Shield to the left and the Mountains to the right was a vast scorched wedge of devastation. 'My feeding grounds,' declared Naiginn with a sweep of his arm.

Torak's gorge rose. The ice demon had carved himself the perfect existence. While his 'Chosen Ones' cowered in their shelters, he could slip from his cave and roam his domain, preying on the dying and the dead.

'But you're still not free,' Torak said quietly. 'Your souls remain bound by your mother's spell.'

'She *lied* to me!' shouted Naiginn. 'She never said there was another way to break it, I found that out for myself!'

His scarred face twisted. 'Dead meat only gives me the *taste* of souls, I need living flesh! Every fluttering, struggling spirit makes me stronger, it loosens my bonds!'

'So why are you still trapped in a mortal body?'

'Not for much longer.'

'You'd better hope so, because you're making mistakes.'

Naiginn turned on him. 'I *never* make mistakes!'

Again his vanity was pricked: he needed to know what Torak meant.

'Every time you venture into your "feeding grounds",' Torak said calmly, 'you leave traces. You can't help it because you know nothing about tracking, nothing about the Forest. You know less than I did when I was five.'

'And you're just talking to keep yourself alive!'

'Maybe. But that bear you slaughtered: you left a footprint beside it.'

Naiginn's chalky eyelashes flickered.

'I knew at once it was yours,' Torak went on. 'And if I spotted that, others will too. It's only a matter of time before you make more mistakes. Before your own people start asking questions—'

'I never make mistakes!' roared Naiginn, flinging Torak to the ground.

Torak fell with winding force, his grunt almost expelling the flint flake from his mouth. He tongued it back in place as the echoes of Naiginn's roars died away.

The ice demon stood over him, breathing unevenly. Suddenly he laughed. 'Clever. Making me shout, hoping my people will hear? Well, what if they do? They'll never turn against *me*! I could slaughter a whole herd of their precious black horses right in front of them – and they'd *still* bow down and call me Leader! Do you know why? Because I give them what they want! *I* am the Great Leader! *I* saved them from the Thunderstar.'

'We both know that's a lie.'

'What do I care? It's what they believe! This is *my* time! *Ice* holds the Forest in its grip!'

'But for how long? With every day the sun grows stronger.'

Naiginn's eyes darkened with fury. 'The Great Demon in the sky sent the Thunderstar to help *me*! With every spirit I devour, my power grows! Soon I will break free of my bonds! I will be perfected, I will be *stronger* than the sun!' He was panting, his lips flecked with greasy foam.

'Poor Naiginn,' mocked Torak. 'It still rankles that you can't do Magecraft.'

'I have greater power than any Mage!'

'No, you don't, you're afraid of them! That's why you turned your people against their Mages. If they hadn't been killed they'd have sniffed you out in a heartbeat! That's why you're after Renn: because she has the power you lack!'

With a supreme effort Naiginn brought himself under control. His white face cracked in a death's-head grin. 'You're the one who's mistaken. I no longer need the girl. I already have her power.'

From inside his robes he drew a band of buckskin and dangled it over his captive.

Torak's heart contracted. It was Renn's belt. 'If – you really had her,' he faltered, 'where's the rest of her gear?'

Naiginn bent closer, his ice-blue stare piercing Torak's. 'She had it on her when she tried to escape,' he murmured. 'When she fell through the ice. And drowned.'

TWENTY-ONE

Wolf had once saved his pack-brother by chasing a herd of bison at a bad tailless. He suspected the pack-sister was trying the same thing now, by chasing the black horses towards the great Den of the White Taillesses.

She was waving her arms at the herd and Wolf was darting around nipping their heels, making sure they went the right way. It was almost as good as hunting with his mate, except that the pack-sister was so slow he had to keep doubling back to check she hadn't got lost.

She made up for that by being *extremely* clever: by snagging a mare's foot with the tree-root, she'd slowed down the whole herd enough so that she could just about keep up.

But they still hadn't reached the Den of the White Taillesses. As the Light swallowed the Dark, Wolf loped uphill, while below him the horses laboured through drifts, the mare snorting with anger because she couldn't kick free of her hobble, the pack-sister plodding behind.

Wolf crested the ridge and cast about wildly. Trees were groaning in the rising wind, Bright Soft Cold swirling down from the Up.

But Wolf couldn't catch the one voice he longed to hear.

'She didn't have time to put on Death Marks,' taunted Naiginn. 'The river scattered her souls. By now she'll be a ghost or a demon, maybe a Lost One.'

'Unless she tricked you,' said Torak without much hope. It was a bluff. He had no idea if Renn was dead or alive.

Wind was keening through the cave, blowing snow around the ice demon as he prowled his lair. Torak half-stood, half-crouched, his wrist still tied to his ankle. Naiginn enjoyed seeing him humiliated.

This will end soon, Torak told himself. If Renn was truly gone, it was all over for him. He'd sooner fling himself down the frozen waterfall than let Naiginn get to work with his knife.

Faint and far, Wolf's howl reached him.

Naiginn halted, his scarred face rigid.

Wolf sounded excited, Torak couldn't make out what

he was saying. He forced a smile. 'Pity you don't know wolf talk.'

'Your wolf can't help you,' sneered Naiginn. 'He tried, he failed. He ran away.'

'So? Even if you're right – if Renn's dead and Wolf can't help – what then? You think I'm going to beg for my life? Is that why you're keeping me alive? You need me to tell you you're the greatest, most powerful being in the Forest – instead of some ugly little demon who scuttled out of a hole in the ice.'

Naiginn snorted, but the barb had shot home.

'Everything about you,' Torak went on, 'is a sham. You can dress up in all the bearskins you like, but you'll never have the power you say you have. I'm the spirit walker. If I become bear, I do it for real.'

'But you'd never dare,' Naiginn said scornfully. 'They say when the bear killed your father, you ran like a hare.'

Torak ignored that. 'I'm the spirit walker, not you – and you can't stand that! I have the power you lack.'

Naiginn twitched. 'You're trying to make me angry. Trying to goad me into killing you quickly. Scared of the pain?'

'You'd like me to be scared. You need me weak. Truth is, you're the one who's weak.'

Naiginn turned on him. 'Ask the Chosen Ones if their Leader is weak!' he bellowed.

Again Wolf howled, this time much closer: *I'm coming!*

A noise at the cave mouth. Realvi poked up his head.

'What is it?' snapped Naiginn.

The Swan Clan hunter gulped, his eyes darting between Torak and his Leader. 'Forgive me, Great One, but... something you have to see!'

'Now what do you do?' Torak said softly.

Naiginn didn't reply. Unwilling to risk leaving his captive in the cave, he'd ordered Torak brought down to camp. Torak stood beside him at the head of the throng, still hobbled, Realvi gripping his hair.

All eyes were on the sacred herd. Half-seen through billowing snow, the black horses had halted at the edge of camp. They'd been running, they were snorting and blowing, flinging down their heads to cough. They had no fear of humans because they'd never been hunted, nor of the voiceless dogs who were leaping and twisting at their stakes.

Torak thought fast. This had to be Wolf's doing. Maybe Renn's too? Somehow he had to get close to the horses – which would mean breaking free of Realvi and hobbling twenty paces across the frozen river, in full view of the Chosen Ones who stood gaping at the herd...

What was wrong with that mare? She was side-stepping, showing the whites of her eyes. Her hind foot seemed to be dragging a chunk of wood, maybe she'd got caught in a trap? When she'd cantered into camp the wood had snagged on a log: she couldn't get free.

Three summers before, Torak had spirit walked in one of the sacred horses. Perhaps they would sense this, they might let him get close...

'Steady now,' he called to the mare.

Naiginn had sent a man creeping behind to cut her loose. A kick from her hind hoof sent him flying.

'Steady,' Torak called again. To Naiginn: 'I wouldn't try that again, she'll kill someone.'

The mare swivelled her ears at his voice, flaring her nostrils to catch his scent. She squealed: didn't like the smell of blood on him. Rearing, bucking, she yanked her foot free of the log. But then, still dragging the hated root, she trotted across the frozen river towards Torak.

The rest of the herd came with her. Awestruck Chosen Ones parted to let them through. For an instant Realvi's grip on Torak's hair slackened and he twisted loose.

'Catch him!' commanded Naiginn.

No one stirred. Already Torak was among the herd, surrounded by steaming flanks and tufted manes, soft strong noses whiffling in his face.

'Shoot him!' cried Naiginn.

But none dared obey for fear of harming the sacred horses.

'Steady now,' Torak told the mare. Blowing gently on her neck to reassure her, he ran his free hand over her back, her rump, and down her leg to her hind foot. His heart leapt. The snare was made from Renn's bowstring, he was sure of it. That must mean she was still alive.

'I'll soon have her free,' he called to the Chosen Ones.

Naiginn had snatched a spear and was trying to take aim.

Swiftly, Torak spat the flint flake into his hand and cut his bonds, then loosened the bowstring round the mare's fetlock and slipped it over her hoof.

The instant before she realized she was free, he scrambled onto her back and dug in his heels.

TWENTY-TWO

Clever pack-sister, her plan was working! Tall Tailless was escaping on the mare, who was galloping with fresh vigour now that she was no longer hindered by that root – and Wolf was racing after them, narrowing his eyes at the chunks of Bright Hard Cold kicked up by flying hooves, overjoyed that his pack-brother was free.

The horses seemed to know exactly where they were going, and the Den of White Taillesses was left far behind as they thundered up the frozen Fast Wet. After plodding at the pack-sister's pace for so long, Wolf revelled in loping at full stretch, with the wind in his fur and the rich scents of the herd streaming over his nose.

The pack-sister had also been left behind. The last

time Wolf had seen her she'd been hiding near the Den of White Taillesses, watching Tall Tailless escape. Wolf hated leaving her. Maybe the White Taillesses were hunting her with the pale-pelted demon who smelt of bear...

A fallen oak barred the way. Like a black torrent the herd flowed over it, Wolf scrambling in the rear.

The frozen Fast Wet came to an end. A steep-sided valley ahead, with twisted rowans and pines. The horses slowed to a trot, picking their way over rocks. Wolf's pelt prickled with unease. This narrow valley smelt strange, and yet he sensed that he'd been here before.

Until now, the horses had shied from him in alarm – but to his surprise, in this valley they were unafraid, merely flattening their ears if he got too close.

Other prey in this place also had no fear. An elk emerged from a thicket and crossed right in front of Wolf's nose, her shaggy calf tottering after her without a backwards glance.

Wolf felt an odd, deep humming in his bones. Then it came to him: this valley belonged to the prey. Here they were safe, they had no fear of hunters. And the trees were the most wakeful he'd ever encountered.

On they went up the shadowy valley. Wolf paused and glanced back. He was worried about the pack-sister. Was she still following? Or had the White Taillesses and the pale-pelted demon captured her?

Up ahead, the last horse disappeared round a bend. Wolf ran to catch up. He had to stay with Tall Tailless and keep him safe. Surely the pack-sister could look after herself?

The trees came to an end. Wolf caught a nose-biting stink of charred Forest: burnt lands ahead. Nothing here was left alive, except the black horses moving between sooty rocks and dead trees.

A chill wind ruffled Wolf's fur. The mare was some lopes ahead, Tall Tailless still clinging to her back. Wolf longed to follow.

But the pack-sister needed him more.

Torak clung to the mare's sweaty, foam-flecked neck. His legs were screaming for rest. He didn't know how much longer he could stay on.

The mare was tiring too. Jolting to a halt, she bucked, sending him flying over her head. He landed with a whump! in a drift of ash-grey snow. The mare flicked up her tail and cantered off, the herd clattering after her.

It was very quiet after the horses had gone. A stink of ash. Icy wind blowing snow in his face. For the first time since he'd been captured by the Chosen Ones, he felt the visceral tug beneath his ribs, much sharper than before.

Getting to his feet, he saw that he stood at the rim of a vast hollow. Within it lay long, uncanny mounds covered in snow. Beyond the hollow rose the High Mountains: glaring white peaks beneath a slatey sky. No birds. No tracks in the snow. Not even the sacred horses of the Deep Forest dared remain in this desolate place.

None of it looked familiar, and yet Torak sensed that he'd been here before. He recognized the strange deep humming in his bones. What *was* this place?

He reached for his medicine horn, then remembered: the Chosen Ones had taken it. A crackling in his ears, the black web hardening around him.

The snow had closed in stealthily, the peaks were gone. At their feet, through the drifting whiteness, he made out a massive rockfall. Something told him it had once been a shoulder of the mountains, now reduced to rubble. A dreadful suspicion took hold.

Snow has the power to alter and conceal – but not for long. It came to Torak that the weird long mounds before him were the ruins of enormous trees. They had all fallen one way, toppled by the same cataclysm that had destroyed that spur.

In his mind Torak saw the Thunderstar smashing into the spur and shattering it to fragments, the explosion felling these giant trees and radiating outwards, devastating a huge expanse of the Forest beyond...

He started climbing over the fallen trees. He had to reach what had once stood within their sheltering arms.

Burnt bark crumbled beneath his boots. He found a twig that still bore a leaf, blackened but intact. Holly.

Scrambling over the last of the prone trunks, he reached the centre of the hollow. Two fallen giants lay side by side. Their root discs towered. Their charcoal trunks, stripped of branches, were studded with rocks embedded by the blast.

The pain under his ribs twisted like a knife. No, no, no.

Torak sank to his knees before what remained of the Great Oak and the Great Yew. The Thunderstar had destroyed the sacred grove. It had obliterated the heart of the Forest.

Wolf was back in the living Forest, racing between pines as he sought the scent of the pack-sister amid its confusion of smells.

Emerging from a thicket, he swerved to avoid a patch of matted branches that smelt suspiciously of White Tailless; he guessed it was one of those pits they dug for catching deer. A few lopes on, he dodged another, and another.

Suddenly he forgot about the pits. Like a kick in the flank, it came to him that something was terribly wrong with Tall Tailless.

Skittering to a halt, Wolf wondered what to do. He felt his pack-brother's horror, his deep, tearing grief.

But now something was getting between them: a horrible crackling. The link snapped. Wolf could no longer sense Tall Tailless at all.

What should Wolf do? Far ahead he heard the pack-sister trudging through the Bright Soft Cold. She was all by herself, she needed him. But from the next valley he caught the scrape of sliding trees and the pant and patter of dogs. Wolf's hackles rose. Snuffing the wind, he smelt the pale-pelted demon. The demon was hunting Tall Tailless with dogs.

Wolf had to save his pack-brother from the demon, it was what Wolf was *for*. Turning tail, he raced back the way he'd come.

He'd only gone a few lopes when the ground beneath his paws snapped and he fell with a thud, hurting his shoulder and bumping his nose.

He was at the bottom of a hole, staring up at a patch of dim grey Up. He leapt, scrabbling at the hole's rocky sides, leapt again. Too high, too steep.

A whine scratched Wolf's throat. He had fallen into one of the pits of the White Taillesses. He couldn't get out.

Torak was on his knees before the wreck of the Great Yew.

Three summers before, he had spirit walked in its golden blood: he had known what it was to be as ancient as the Forest itself. The Yew had been a seedling at the thawing of the Great Cold, a sapling at the coming of the Great Wave. For thousands of winters it had endured. Now it was dead.

Torak had been born inside its huge hollow trunk, which lay broken before him. The Yew had been his mother's Death Tree, it held her bones. Before she died, she'd buried the navel-cord of her infant son in its embrace. That was the tug Torak had been feeling since the Thunderstar struck.

Heartstone, that's the most vital of all, the Walker had said. *In the deepest deeps of the Deep Forest they will find it...* Torak had known from the start that this meant the sacred grove. Now he was here, and there was nothing left. No green heartstone, nothing but black. The Thunderstar had murdered green.

The last drop of hope drained from his spirit like blood into sand. There would be no four arrows and no Rite. The First Tree would never return.

The Forest would die.

TWENTY-THREE

There had been times while Dark was living in the Mountains when he'd lost all hope. He would never see another human being again, he would live out his life alone.

At such times the only thing that had helped had been to concentrate on *now*: on the heat of the fire and the chewy mountain hare, on Ark blinking with pleasure as he stroked her scaly foot. Sometimes this had cheered him up, sometimes not. Always it had given him just enough strength to carry on.

He was doing it again as he unrolled his sleeping-sack in his deadwood shelter among the pines. It wasn't working. It was ages since he'd said goodbye to Fin-Kedinn, and the camp of the Red Deer Clan felt like a different world, and despite their careful directions about how to avoid the Chosen Ones and find the sacred grove, he was lost. He'd tried summoning ghosts to help him, but none had come to his aid.

He was cold too. The Red Deer had told him to gather elk droppings because in winter they're full of bark and burn without smoke. Trouble was, Dark couldn't find any. Torak would be able to tell at a glance if elk had passed this way, but after only three summers in the Forest, Dark had a job distinguishing elk tracks from deer.

What was he *doing* here? How had he *imagined* he could make his way through this hostile, unknowable *Deep* Forest, *and* find Torak and Renn, *and* do the Rite? It was impossible. It had always been impossible.

'Come on, Dark,' he muttered. 'Still light for a while, let's go and find something to eat.'

He was about to move the branches from the entrance when he heard a noise outside. Something big crunching through the snow.

The Red Deer had warned him about Skin-Takers. Once in the night he'd lain in a cold sweat, fancying he heard footsteps. He was hearing them now. Slow, heavy. Unafraid.

Whatever it was grunted. A snuffling noise. Not a Skin-Taker. Dark's mind flew to boar, bison…

Bear.

He waited, heart bumping in his chest, not daring to peer out.

The creature was coming towards the shelter. Dark cast about for his axe. He'd left it outside against a tree. His bow and slingstones would be useless, knife scarcely better, the bear would simply bat it away.

It reached the shelter and stopped. Definitely bear, he could tell by the smell. Nothing to protect him but this flimsy arrangement of branches.

More snufflings. The shelter shook. Dark pictured one massive paw swatting this odd pile of branches that smelt curiously human.

Then, poking through: the bear's long brown muzzle. Dark felt its hot rank breath, he saw its purple-grey tongue, its glistening yellow fangs.

Feverishly he wrenched open his medicine pouch, shook earthblood into his palm. Taking a deep breath, he blew a red cloud at the bear's nose.

Its muzzle sharply withdrew – Dark heard a colossal sneeze – snow was spattering the shelter. When he dared look, he saw the bear's furry hindquarters disappearing into the pines.

Shakily he crawled outside and lurched to his feet. He gave an edgy laugh. He retched till his belly ached.

The day was on the turn, the sky a livid mauve, heavy with snow. The demon time: when courage fails and hope dies.

Dark watched a flock of crows speeding over the treetops on their way to roost. Their diminishing caws made him feel lonelier than ever. If only Ark would come and perch on his shoulder. If only he'd brought Spike. He missed the young hedgehog's scratchy warmth inside his jerkin, the way she politely flattened her bristles when he picked her up.

'What am I doing here?' he asked the cold sky.

His belly rumbled. His provisions were gone and he'd seen nothing but lemmings all day.

'Mushrooms,' he said briskly.

In the failing light he found a few lurid blue ones that shouted poison, and several lookalikes he wasn't sure about. The only ones he felt confident in gathering were the squidgy black blobs the clans called 'demon droppings'.

Back in the shelter, he ate one. It tasted as disgusting as it looked. He bit another. It crunched. The piece he was holding contained a beetle's back end. He swallowed what was in his mouth and chucked the rest.

He woke from a doze he'd never meant to have to the dreadful certainty that something was moving around outside. Oh, not again.

This time he'd remembered to bring his axe inside. Clutching it in icy fingers, he waited.

Was it a bear? Whatever it was, it was making no attempt at stealth as it approached the shelter. A Chosen One? A demon?

Branches fell outwards and a hooded head peered in.

'Dark?' said Renn.

'How did you find me?' said Dark, grinning from ear to ear.

'Followed Ark,' said Renn. 'When she perched on top of the shelter I was pretty sure it was you. I'm hungry, let's eat, then we can work out what to do.'

She offered him reindeer tongues from her pouch and watched in surprise as he fell on them as if he hadn't eaten in days. Like her he was smeared in chalk, but as he was always pale and his hair already white, he looked reassuringly unchanged, although she could tell that at first he'd been taken aback by her own grey hair.

She asked what he'd been finding to eat and he mumbled something about demon droppings. She choked. 'You *didn't*!'

He nodded.

'What do they taste like?'

'What d'you think?'

They burst into jittery laughter.

The shelter hardly had space enough for them both, but after creeping through the Forest in terror of Naiginn and the Chosen Ones, Renn thought it was wonderful.

'I'm *so* glad to see you,' Dark said simply.

'Me too! But how did you *get* here?'

'Red Deer Clan. To begin with they wouldn't help, but then they saw Ark. They said she's like First Raven before he stole the sun, which meant they *had* to help.'

She rolled her eyes. 'That sounds like them.'

His grin faded. 'My father's a spy. He was sent to find

out if you and Torak survived the Thunderstar. He and his fellow spies slunk back to tell their leader—'

'Naiginn,' she declared.

He stared at her. 'You know?'

'I've seen him.'

'Did you see... Realvi?'

She nodded. 'In their camp, just before Torak got away.' She told him about watching from the trees: Naiginn in his bearskins, Torak galloping off on the black mare. 'Naiginn was furious that no one dared shoot the horses, but he turned it to his advantage, said it proved the Chosen Ones are still stuck in the old ways and need him even more.'

She picked a shred of meat from between her teeth. 'Dark, I've a feeling he made up the Skin-Takers. When Torak and I were with the Red Deer we heard a weird up-and-down roaring. The Red Deer said it was Skin-Takers, but I wonder if it wasn't Naiginn. Maybe he invented the whole thing to keep people in their shelters while he raids corpses. I had a dream... I think he believes that if he eats enough head meat, he can break the spell.'

Dark was nodding slowly. 'D'you think it'll work?'

'I don't know. What I do know is he wants me and Torak dead.' She paused. 'Right now he's after Torak. The horses headed up the sacred river. The Chosen Ones are following on foot, they didn't dare take dog sleds – but Naiginn's a demon, he doesn't care.'

'Aren't dogs scared of him?'

'Terrified, but it makes them run faster.'

They fell silent, listening to the creak of pines, snow pattering onto the shelter.

'Those weird sounds you heard,' Dark said in a low voice. 'I think I know what made them.'

She looked at him.

'Mountain people call them bull-roarers. We make them to summon spirits. You take a flat piece of wood about a hand long, tie on a length of sinew, whirl it round and round.' His mouth set. 'Realvi would know all about them.'

'You talk as if he's a stranger.'

His pale features had gone as hard as quartz. 'I will never call him my father again.'

'You can't choose your parents, Dark. I know that better than most.'

He did not respond. 'Before we head out I'll make a couple of bull-roarers. They might help frighten off the Chosen Ones.'

'You think we should go now?'

'Renn, there's no time to waste, it's the third night of the moon's dark!'

The Rite. She'd been so overjoyed at finding him that she'd almost forgotten why they were here. 'Then it's all over,' she burst out. 'We haven't got a single arrow, we can't do the Rite!'

'Um – I have these.' Pulling a salmon-skin bundle from his quiver, he unwrapped the most extraordinary arrows Renn had ever seen. One had a head of Sea-blue crystal, another of lucent scarlet; the third was as clear as ice.

'I made that one on the way,' he explained. 'Fletched it with a white owl feather Torak gave me before you left. I've brought the makings for the fourth arrow: dogwood shaft, green woodpecker feathers, deer sinew, birch-bark tar. But if we can't find the heartstone – whatever that is – then—'

'Dark, you're *amazing!* I didn't think we had *any!*'

A flush stole across his cheekbones.

'Problem is,' Renn went on, 'the Chosen Ones broke my bow.'

'The Red Deer gave me one. See what you think.'

Renn took the bow in silence. It was the perfect length and it fitted her grip as if it was made for her. Fashioned of well-seasoned yew, its back was of flexible sapwood, its belly of stronger heartwood. And like only the very best bow wood, it was dense and fine-grained; this told Renn it had come from some deep valley where the trees had to fight for light.

'They gave me this too.' Dark handed her a small rawhide pouch. 'They said it's special oil, won't freeze in the coldest weather.'

'From reindeer foot-joints,' murmured Renn. Reverently she ran her finger over the bowstring of taut, twisted sinew, while silently apologizing to the Red Deer for every ungenerous comment she'd ever made about them.

Dark was watching her anxiously. 'Isn't it good enough?'

She was too choked to reply. Crawling outside, she nocked one of Dark's ordinary arrows to the bow and aimed at the topmost pine cone on the tallest tree she could see.

The bow was perfectly strung for the quietest action: the arrow shot straight and true, hitting the target, then arching into a snowdrift. Renn retrieved it, plucked the pine cone from the tip, walked back to Dark.

He stood with his mouth open. 'That was the most incredible shot I've ever seen.'

'This,' she declared, 'is the best bow I have *ever* had the honour to shoot. Not even the one Fin-Kedinn made for me after Fa died came close – and I *never* thought I'd say that. Dark, you're not just amazing, you're...' She flung her arms wide. '*This* much amazing!'

He was smiling, scuffing the snow with his boot. 'Then you'd better keep it. Take my quiver. So... apart from the heartstone, what else do we need for the Rite?'

She furrowed her brow, trying to recall what the Walker had said. *The Voice of Then becomes the Song of Now...*

'I've wondered about that. Do you think—'

'My mammut-bone flute? Thing is, I don't know how to play.'

'I do.' When she looked surprised he shrugged. 'Seven winters on my own. It was something to do.'

'Here, take it. What about *the brightest souls in the Forest?*'

He shook his head. 'I've thought and thought.'

All her doubts came rushing back. By the slump of his shoulders, Dark felt the same way. 'And even if we had everything,' he said, 'we've no idea *where* to do it. I don't even know where we are.'

'Neither do I. I was tracking the horses up what I *think*

was the sacred river, but I had to hide from the Chosen Ones, I got lost. I don't know the way to the sacred grove.' She had a sudden thought. *'Some places in the Forest you can only find when you're lost...* D'you think that means here?'

'No,' said Dark in an altered voice. He was gazing intently at a stand of pines ten paces away.

Without a word, he left Renn and walked towards the trees. Something warned her not to follow. In the blink of an eye, Dark had changed from a modest and kindly boy to the Mage who talked to ghosts.

It had stopped snowing, and the twilit sky glowed a deep clear purple. The Forest was very still, the pines wide awake, watching. Renn shivered. The third night of the moon's dark was about to begin.

Starlight and snowglow glittered on her friend's long white hair as he bowed to someone she couldn't see. Her spine tingled. Her hand crept to her clan-creature feathers. They were daubed with chalk, and it flashed across her mind that this might stop them protecting her.

Dark was talking quietly to the unseen presence. 'I don't want to offend you,' he said calmly. 'But we are living people – so, please, don't come any closer.'

He fell silent, nodding as if in response. Then said: 'Yes, we came to do the Rite to bring back the First Tree – but we can't find the place. Can any of you help?'

What? thought Renn. How many ghosts were there?

Another pause, Dark turning his head this way and

that, as if listening to several voices. Now he was bowing, thanking the invisible throng.

His face was clear as he walked back to Renn, and he was pointing uphill. 'That way,' he said.

TWENTY-FOUR

Wolf had broken his claws and scraped his pads raw from leaping at the pit's stony sides. He'd tried and tried. He still couldn't get out.

He'd howled, but Tall Tailless hadn't howled back – and even worse, Wolf couldn't feel his spirit at all. The last he'd sensed of his pack-brother had been grief and despair. Now Tall Tailless was lost behind a dense confusion of roots.

Wolf was thirsty. He snapped at the Bright Soft Cold falling from the Up. It didn't help. Unable to pace, he turned round and round. Hunger gnawed his belly. He heard lemmings pattering through their tunnels. From the next valley he caught the muzzle-watering scent of reindeer.

The wind changed, carrying the noisy footsteps of

taillesses. Hope leapt: were Tall Tailless and the pack-sister coming to his rescue?

Hope died as Wolf smelt White Taillesses. Two of them: one with a faint scent of bat, the other of horse.

His hackles bristled. In his chest a growl began. They were coming towards him.

Two heads peered down at him. Wolf sprang, snapping and snarling. The horse-smelling tailless was scrawny and scared, the bat-smelling one merely wary.

They disappeared, but Wolf could hear that they hadn't gone far. After much grunting and puffing they returned with a beech sapling, which – to Wolf's astonishment – they lowered into the pit. He yelped as its trunk squashed his forepaw. What were they *doing*?

The taillesses were blinking at him expectantly, the bat-tailless talking in quiet respectful tones. Wolf was puzzled. Were they trying to *help*? But White Taillesses were *bad*, they hunted his pack-brother and -sister...

Suddenly he remembered the White Taillesses bowing to him in awe. He sniffed the trunk propped against the side of the pit. Cautiously, he tried to climb it. Too steep, too smooth, he couldn't do it.

The White Taillesses hauled it out. When they returned – more grunting – they brought a pine. It was thicker, with snapped-off branches and good rough bark: *much* better. In a snap Wolf scrambled up it and fled.

The *relief* of being out of that horrible pit, with the wind in his fur and Bright Soft Cold cooling his sore paws!

Something made him turn and glance back.

The two taillesses were kneeling by the pit, grinning and slapping each other's shoulders. The bat-tailless spotted Wolf and spoke to the other. They gazed at him open-muzzled.

Holding his head high, Wolf returned their gaze, gave a slight twitch of his tailtip. He didn't know if they understood that he was thanking them, but they were still grinning when he raced off into the Forest.

The last of the Light was leaving the trees and a flock of crows was flying overhead as he sped uphill to catch the scents. At the top he put up his muzzle and howled to Tall Tailless: *Where – are – you?*

Still no reply. Worry sank its teeth into his belly.

Darkness is tugging at Torak's souls. He is caught in a crackling chaos of roots.

Dimly through the black web he becomes aware of the muffled cawing of crows: growing louder as they fly over, then rapidly fading.

A pecking sound, much nearer. Torak wants to look, but his eyelids are made of stone.

Peck-peck-peck!

…With an enormous effort he opened his eyes.

It was night. The sky was clear. No moon, the first stars coming out. It took him a moment to remember where he was: in what remained of the sacred grove, on his knees before the ruins of the Great Yew.

Three ravens perched on its trunk. Rip and Rek glanced at him, then went on pecking. The third raven was white. Torak cast about. Did this mean Renn was here? And Dark?

He couldn't see anyone. Beyond the ravaged grove rose the rockfall – and beyond that, the Mountains' looming bulk. He longed to howl for Wolf – but the black web held him fast.

Ark! croaked the white raven, fixing him with her bright black eyes. She flew to a clump of rocks near the wreck of the Great Oak. She wanted him to follow. He couldn't summon the will.

Ark dipped her head, cawing encouragement.

Somehow Torak forced himself to his feet and shuffled towards her. The white raven was peering into a gap between two large rocks, blinking rapidly, gurgling with delight.

Torak blinked too. Tucked between the rocks and covered in soot, a seedling had survived the blast.

Shakily he brushed it clean. Two stiff twigs bristled with tiny needles. If it lived, it would become a yew.

Deep within Torak, hope flickered. If this seedling could survive, then maybe...

Far to the south, beyond what remained of the sacred grove, he made out living treetops pricking the stars. His heart contracted. All his life the Forest had protected him. It had given him everything he needed to survive. Now *it* needed *him*.

He couldn't wait for Renn or Dark, there was no time left. He wasn't a Mage, and he had nothing with which to perform the Rite – but if there was even a chance of bringing back the First Tree, he had to take it.

The Walker's voice sounded in his mind: *Heartstone, that's the most vital of all...* What if, somewhere in this devastation, a fragment of heartstone had survived?

Even if Torak never saw Renn or Wolf again – even if his spirit was ripped apart in the attempt – he had to try. He had to risk annihilation by spirit walking in the Forest's teeming souls.

He had to ask it to help him find the heartstone.

The seedling was the only living tree within reach, so Torak would have to spirit walk in that, and hope to be swept into the souls of older, wiser trees who might tell him how to find what he sought.

In this lay his chance – and also lethal danger. Three summers ago he had learnt that trees aren't separate but linked, when his souls had been swept through the Forest... *The Voice of the Forest,* Durrain had told him afterwards, *is too vast for men to bear. If you'd heard it for more than a heartbeat your souls would have been torn apart...*

If this went wrong, he might become a ghost or a demon – or even a Lost One, cut off for ever from all living things, drifting alone in infinite blackness beyond the stars.

'No time to lose,' he muttered. Besides, if Durrain had never heard the Voice, how could she know for sure?

He had no potion to loosen his souls, so on impulse he broke off a charred flake of the Great Oak's bark. He put it in his mouth and chewed. An image came to him of Renn last spring, doing a charm to find prey: her red hair had been vivid against the fresh green bracken, her face grave and intent as she chewed oak bark...

...and suddenly the wind was scraping his twigs against the rock and his roots were clinging determinedly to the frozen earth.

The seedling was still getting used to being alive, and though it missed its great fallen mother, and the oak and the guardian hollies, it wasn't afraid, for it was not alone: it was cradled by an immense, murmuring mesh of souls. But *what* was this strange speck of not-tree hiding in its stem?

Silently Torak told it what he sought – and with startling strength the seedling thrust him out through its rootlets and sent him hurtling into an endless turmoil of roots – some dead, some dying, others stubbornly alive – from ash to holly to rowan to lime, past the moist coils of sleeping worms, the furry warmth of snoring badgers ... up groaning trunks, through thrashing branches, into buds tight-furled for spring.

'I have to find a piece of the heartstone!' he cried.

But the trees were lost in pain, their many-fingered hands searching the sky for the First Tree that gave them life – and finding only darkness and icy, uncaring stars.

Why should they heed this frail human when the Forest was dying?

How, wondered Torak, could he make them listen, when his spirit was as insignificant as a bat-squeak in a storm?

He found himself in the stony foot of a fierce old pine which held demons fast in its grip. Their sharp cruel faces leered at him, snapping at his souls... With a cry he leapt from the root into the trunk, and up through the surging thickness of the pine's golden blood.

Suddenly Torak realized that *he* had made that leap, not the pine! Despite his fear, he felt wild elation. No man knows what it is to be tree, they are the deepest of mysteries, eating only sunlight, growing a new limb if one is lost – but Torak was learning their secrets...

Next moment he lost control, tumbling into a beechling that was about to be crushed by a bison's hoof. With a yelp he jumped into a rowan, landing in a berry, frost-crusted, trembling in the wind.

The berry dipped and bobbed: a mistle thrush leant forwards to peck it. Torak escaped being eaten by dropping into a lower branch.

He felt the weight of a human hand. Dark was gripping the branch to steady himself as he adjusted his snowshoe.

Torak caught Renn's junipery scent: his branch had snagged a lock of her hair. She freed herself – then spun round, startled, eyes wide. Had she sensed him?

Too soon he was snatched away. Now he was drowning

in tree-souls, the Voice of the Forest rising, wanting him gone.

'I'm trying to *save* you!' he cried.

You cannot... whispered the vast awareness, rising, swelling to an unbearable roar that would tear him apart.

In desperation he shouted: 'I have spirit walked in the oldest of trees! I have known the souls of the Great Yew!'

Silence. Space opening around him, the Forest falling away, stars rushing to meet him – then he was spiralling down, down into a ring of ancient trees. An ash squat as a boulder, a huge headless oak with branches sprouting from its belly, a beech split in half by a long-ago storm, but still alive. Their branches and roots intertwined, and as one being they perceived the fragile human spirit cowering in their blood.

To Torak's astonishment he sensed a leafy rustle of mirthless laughter. *Why do you ask us for what you seek? The answer already lies within your grasp!*

'What do you mean?' he pleaded.

More grim laughter.

And deep in their golden blood, the spark that was Torak faltered...

...and understood.

TWENTY-FIVE

'Torak, wake up!' Renn shook him by the shoulders. 'Please, Torak, come back to me!'

He lay face down beside the trunk of the Great Yew: terrifyingly still in the glimmer of Dark's rushlight, one fist clenched tight.

Dark put his fingertips under Torak's jaw. 'Still alive, but his souls are far away, he's in a trance.'

'Spirit walking,' said Renn, remembering the odd impression she'd had at the rowan tree that Torak was somewhere very close. If her guess was correct and his souls had been in the trees, he must be still out there. 'Oh, Torak, how will you ever get back?'

Dark turned him over. Renn gasped. 'What did Naiginn

do to you?' she cried. Torak's lips were flecked with foam, his right cheek crusted with blood.

'What's he got in his fist?' said Dark.

'What does that matter?' she snapped.

'It's a stone. Look, that's where he dug it out of the trunk.' He sucked in his breath. 'It's so heavy, I can feel its power. Renn, I think... I think it's a piece of the Thunderstar!'

Dragging her gaze from Torak, Renn stared at the dull grey stone on Dark's palm. Her mind flew back to the moments after the Thunderstar struck: charred tree-trunks studded with rocks embedded by the blast. Her eyes went to the looming mass of the rockfall. She pictured the Thunderstar smashing into the mountainside, exploding in a million fragments...

Dark was peering intently at the stone. 'What's inside you?' he whispered.

Before she knew what he was doing, he'd set it on a boulder, grabbed a rock with both hands and brought it crashing down on the stone. He shouted in triumph. 'Renn, look! Torak *found* it! He found the heartstone!'

The stone had split in two, revealing a crystalline heart of unearthly green fire. Renn swallowed. Torak had longed to see green again – and now he wasn't here to see this. His spirit was wandering alone, lost in the Forest. It wasn't fair.

Dark was jubilant. 'I can work this stone, I know I can! I can make the fourth arrow!'

Dark said the heartstone knew its destiny, it wouldn't take him long to make the arrow.

Renn hardly heard him. She was doing everything she could to protect Torak: chewing pine-pitch from her medicine pouch to soften it, patting the poultice gently on his cheek; rubbing her palms fast and hard together, then holding them over his chest to lend him some of her power.

Dark touched her arm. 'The arrow's done, we have to go.'

'Not yet.'

'Right now,' he said sternly.

'You call yourself his friend?'

'Renn, I've told you this is not the place to do the Rite!'

'But he's *helpless*! What if the Chosen Ones find him? Or Naiginn?'

Earlier they'd had to use their bull-roarers to frighten off a band of Chosen Ones. The Chosen Ones had been on foot, Renn guessed they didn't dare bring dogs into the sacred valley, but it wouldn't be long before they caught up; and Naiginn with his dog sled couldn't be far away.

And yet Dark was right, they had to go. Numbly she watched him unroll his sleeping-sack. 'While I'm getting Torak inside,' he said, 'you put marks of power on him – but *hurry*, it's already past middle-night!'

'Where's *Wolf*?' she cried. 'Why isn't he here to protect him?'

'Whistle for him,' Dark said tersely as he eased Torak's inert form into his sleeping-sack.

With trembling lips Renn blew her duckbone whistle, sending the silent summons that only Wolf could hear. No answering howls. To her horror, she caught the distant scrape of a dog sled.

Dark stiffened. 'Naiginn. We've got to go!'

'Wait!' Feverishly she dabbed some of her precious mix of earthblood and mammut ash on Torak's forehead and throat. Then she daubed her ravenfoot mark on his palm, so that if he woke – *when* he woke, she told herself – he would know that she'd done what she could to protect him.

She bent and kissed his mouth. 'I have to leave you,' she whispered. 'I have to do this for all of us – but I *will* see you again!'

'Renn, come *on!*' urged Dark.

With a ragged sob she rose to her feet – threw Torak a last look – and left him lying defenceless in the snow.

With a shock of recognition Torak gazed down at himself lying in the snow. One side of his face was dark with blood. Moments before, Renn had gently pushed back his hair.

He remembered waking briefly after spirit walking in the ring of ancient trees. He'd found himself back in his body, horribly weak, but alight with the knowledge of where to find the heartstone.

Somehow he'd summoned the strength to crawl back to the trunk of the Great Yew – to prise from its bark the pebble which the ravens' pecking had worked loose. This was what the ancient trees had been telling him: *What you seek is already within your grasp...*

After that he remembered nothing, he must have blacked out. Nothing until now, when he found himself watching from the top of a tall pine in the unburnt Forest south of the grove.

He knew that he was spirit walking once more, and yet this time he wasn't being swept from tree to tree, and he no longer dreaded the Voice of the Forest. The trees knew he was trying to save them. This pine was sheltering him, cradling his spirit like a raindrop trembling on a leaf.

With the strange awareness of trees that need no eyes to see, Torak saw Renn and Dark far away. They'd reached the bottom of the rockfall, no longer bothering to brush away their tracks: the time for concealment was past.

He saw Wolf further down the sacred valley, running with his nose to the ground as he followed their scent.

He saw a band of Chosen Ones some way behind Wolf, moving up-valley on foot – and nearer, terrifyingly near, he saw Naiginn.

The ice demon slewed to a halt where the valley became impassable to his sled and continued on foot. He had shed his circlet of bear claws and his cumbersome furs: his parka and leggings were seal-hide, and he was armed with knife, axe, bow and club. Spying Dark's rushlight near the base of the rockfall, he hastened past the fallen hollies without spotting Torak's body.

The wind was rising, the pines swaying and murmuring, sensing the demon's raging hunger to destroy...

Torak *had* to reach Naiginn before he could attack Renn and Dark. He was a long way from the sacred grove, but perhaps by spirit walking from tree to tree he might reach the yew seedling, he might stop Naiginn before it was too late.

His souls were drained of strength. He willed himself to do it...

He couldn't.

He tried again. Not possible. His spirit was too weak, the pine's blood too thick. He was stuck.

TWENTY-SIX

D ark quenched his rushlight in a patch of snow and wished he'd thought of doing that sooner. Why make things easy for Naiginn?

The rockfall reared above him, treacherous with wind-polished ice. Softly he called down to Renn: 'D'you think we've come high enough?'

'Who knows?' she panted. *'Some places you can only find when you're lost*: that could mean anywhere.'

He went on climbing. Since making the fourth arrow his confidence had trickled away. This wasn't going to work. They only had the vaguest idea how to do the Rite, and they hadn't found the brightest souls in the Forest. Hardly likely they'd come across them up here on this shattered mountainside.

Pausing for breath, he was surprised to see how far they'd climbed. Below him the sacred grove was a lake of frost-blue snow netted with the sombre corpses of trees. Where was Naiginn? Never having seen the ice demon, Dark pictured a nightmare creature creeping after them...

A raven sped overhead, wingbeats loud in the stillness; Dark couldn't tell if it was Rip or Rek. A moment later Ark flew past, pale in the gloom. She made to perch on a nearby column of rock, then swerved and settled on his shoulder instead.

The next instant Dark understood why.

'Why'd you stop?' Renn called quietly.

Signing her to silence, he pointed at the rock which Ark had avoided. *Hidden People*, he mouthed.

Somehow the rock had withstood the destruction of the mountainside. Unseen hands had righted it, unseen hands had hammer-pecked a warning on its frost-crusted face: three tall stick-thin figures standing with skeletal arms flung wide.

Dark's heart thudded in his chest. Now what?

Renn came up behind him, her eyes and mouth shadowy pits in her chalk-white face.

Dark turned back to the rock. He bowed. Quietly he addressed what dwelt within. 'I don't want to disturb you. But know that I kept faith with your kin, the Hidden People of the Caves—'

'We know.' A voice as harsh as granite: he couldn't tell if it spoke out loud or in his mind.

'Please,' he begged. 'Let us pass! We seek the place to do the Rite, to summon back the First Tree!'

Renn sucked in her breath. 'Look!'

The hammer-pecked figures were detaching from the rock. Half-glimpsed in the gloom they floated, like the grainy shapes Dark saw when he shut his eyes: now coalescing to near-human form, now breaking apart, melting into the dimness – but always drifting closer.

Dark spread his arms, shielding Renn. The Hidden People were all around, frosty breath chilling his face. Fingers insubstantial as mist pointed up the slope...

The night wind blew snow in Dark's face. The Hidden People were gone. The hammer-etched figures were back on the rock.

'There.' Renn pointed at a huge tilted slab a little further up.

Dark felt a flicker of hope. If the Hidden People had indicated the place, they must think he and Renn had a chance.

'Yes,' he murmured. 'That's where we do the Rite.'

A magpie clattered an alarm call. Torak woke with a start. He was cold. He was high in the sky. *No, no, no!* His spirit was still held immobile in the pine's sticky blood.

The wind had dropped, and he saw his surroundings with the eyeless perception of trees: stars astonishingly bright, frost glinting on the distant rockfall where the tiny figures of Renn and Dark were doggedly climbing. Below them Naiginn was gaining ground.

Torak made one last desperate attempt to free his souls. His efforts took him as far as the pine's trunk. The tree blood was thicker than tar, and though he could move he was horribly slow, he'd never make it in time to help Renn and Dark.

He heard snuffling. A bear was prowling about the pine's roots. Rearing, it raked the trunk with its claws.

Torak thought fast. If he spirit walked in that bear, he might be able to reach Naiginn in time. He could attack with the might of the strongest hunter in the Forest...

Why, *why* did he hesitate? It wasn't the fear of being unable to master the bear's souls, his reluctance cut deeper than that. Suddenly Torak was twelve summers old, crouching in the wreck of the shelter where his father lay dying. Fa was in agony, beseeching Torak to *run* from the creature who would soon tear his life away...

That was why Torak couldn't bring himself to spirit walk in the bear. If he did, his claws would be as vicious as the claws that had gashed Fa's belly – his fangs as savage as those that had torn Fa's flesh from his bones... *No, no, I can't!* screamed Torak in the tree's tarry blood.

Renn had paused on a huge tilted slab of rock, apparently unaware of Naiginn climbing towards her. Wolf was still far down the sacred valley, he wasn't going to reach them in time.

With a roar Torak tore himself from the trunk and leapt into the bear's marrow...

...and though its thoughts were sluggish and simple, its souls were overwhelmingly strong, its feelings a blazing torrent engulfing Torak in rage.

The bear was angry at *everything*! It was angry at the earth for jolting it awake from its beautiful snug Den and thrusting it into the freezing dark. It was angry at the Forest for getting burnt, and at other bears for taking every available hole, leaving it searching in vain for a new Den. And now it was angry at this faint, infuriating scratching in its head, like a gnat whining to get out.

Torak was no longer seeing with the needle-sharp clarity of pines, but with the bear's short-sighted vision: blurry trees, vague hummocks of snow-covered bushes. That didn't matter, he was seeing with his nose. Beyond the tang of scratched bark and bitter ash, he 'saw' an intricate mesh of scents: lichen, lemming, raven, badger, squirrel, deer, horse, dog; the sweat of climbing boy, the tender flesh of girl...

The bear growled. Torak felt his claws tighten. A shudder ran through the massive hump of muscle between his shoulders. The bear smelt demon. The bear *hated* demon.

Now it was galloping downhill, Torak riding inside, revelling in its speed and strength. Startlingly soon they reached the sacred grove, and the bear was hauling itself tirelessly up icy boulders, tracking the demon's foul scent.

For a blunt-minded creature the bear was cunning, keeping downwind of its quarry, finding hidden approaches among rocks, placing its huge pads noiselessly, without a single click of its long claws.

The caws of ravens rang down the valley. Rip, Rek and Ark were calling to each other – and they were calling to another creature too.

The bear hesitated, licking the ravens' scents off the wind. *No*, Torak commanded, *go after Naiginn!*

But the bear was too strong, and from down-valley it had caught a new scent: a creature who was the enemy of all bears...

A wolf.

Wolf raced scornfully past the dogs tied to their sliding tree, scrambled over the fallen hollies, skidded to a halt beside the motionless body of Tall Tailless.

Wolf barked in his pack-brother's ears. Couldn't wake him up. Tall Tailless's Breath-that-Walks was far away, Wolf couldn't sense where.

To his astonishment Wolf smelt that the pack-sister and the friendly pale-pelted tailless had been here only a few snaps ago – *but they had left.* Wolf couldn't believe it. The pack-sister *abandoning* her mate? Leaving him alone, unprotected?

Nothing would make Wolf leave Tall Tailless, not ever ever ever.

But suddenly Wolf smelt demon. It was the demon that had shot him and tried to kill Tall Tailless. Wolf smelt that the demon wasn't hunting his pack-brother, it was heading up the rocks after the pack-sister.

Wolf glanced at Tall Tailless's sleeping form, then at the rocks. He didn't know what to do. He had to stay and protect his pack-brother – but what about the pack-sister? And hunting demons was what Wolf was *for*.

Wolf leapt onto the fallen yew and raced along its trunk to take a look. He saw the demon climbing towards the pack-sister and the pale-pelted tailless – but that wasn't all.

Climbing after them was the enemy of all wolves: a bear.

TWENTY-SEVEN

'Sh! Did you hear that?'
'What?'

'I thought I heard something. Down there…'

Renn and Dark froze, straining for sounds of pursuit.

Nothing. Even the ravens had fallen silent.

The zigzag tattoos on Renn's wrists were stinging. She'd been taking deep breaths and still felt breathless, an ugly pressure on her chest, a thickening in the air. 'Naiginn's not far,' she whispered.

Dark nodded. He'd flung back his hood, starlight gleaming on his pale eyebrows, his cobwebby hair. 'I sense lesser demons too,' he breathed. 'Drawn by his will.'

As if they'd heard him, shadows retreated into the gloom and Renn heard a sly trickle of evil laughter.

The slab on which she and Dark were standing was only three paces wide, with an alarming tilt. Above it more rocks rose skywards. Below stretched the dim slope they'd just climbed.

Hurriedly they purified themselves, rubbing faces and hands with Renn's powdered earthblood and mammut ash. Reluctantly she set aside her axe, then oiled her bow. From now on she must only handle the weapon she would use for the Rite.

Her nerves were as taut as her bowstring, her fingers shook as she arranged the four arrows in her quiver. Settling it on her back, she practised reaching for them. *Four arrows to bring back the First Tree... A bridge of light flying beyond moon and stars... The Voice of Then becomes the Song of Now...*

You'll never do it, sniggered a demon from the rocks.

Rip, Rek and Ark perched above the slab, on the lookout for attack. Dark stood two paces away, gripping the mammut-bone flute, waiting for her to begin. It gave her some comfort that unlike her, he could keep his weapons.

...If the brightest souls in the Forest can sing the arrows on their way, they will bring back the First Tree – and the world will be saved...

But you haven't got the brightest souls, hissed the demon. *It can't possibly work!*

Ark half-opened her snowy wings and bowed to Renn. Rip and Rek did the same, dipping their dusky heads.

The demon slunk away. Renn squared her shoulders.

The ravens were more than companions, they were the spirits of her ancestors, the guardians of her clan.

Again she touched the arrows. Fin-Kedinn had made two of them, she'd recognized his way of tying sinew – and he too was with her. In her mind she heard him teaching her to shoot when she was little: *The vital thing is to concentrate so hard on your target your eyes burn a hole in it...*

For this, the most crucial Magecraft of her life, she had no target, not at the outset: she would shoot the first arrow east over the High Mountains to where the sun was born – and after that her target would be the first arrow, then the one after that, making a bridge that arched across the sky—

Can't be done, snickered the demon. *You know that, why bother trying?*

Dark put the flute to his lips.

She nodded.

Thin music spiralled upwards as she began to chant: *'Blue arrow of the Sea: I have you! Red arrow of the Sun: I have you! White arrow of the snow: I have you! Green arrow of the Forest: I have you! On many-coloured wings I send you to the First, the Greatest of Trees, reaching through the dark beyond the stars to summon it back...'*

Before she could take the first arrow from the quiver, the ravens lifted skywards with rattling alarm calls. Dark went on playing, his eyes begging her to hurry.

Don't try to shut out what's happening, Fin-Kedinn warned her in her mind. *Instead fix your attention on what you're about to do,* see *yourself at every stage, doing each perfectly...*

231

She pictured herself drawing back the bowstring, shooting the arrows so fast they were chasing each other's tails, red after blue, icy-clear and finally green, a rainbow bridge reaching all the way to the lost boughs of the First Tree...

Feet apart at shoulder width, weight evenly placed on both feet, nock the arrow, keep your bow shoulder down... She'd done it ten thousand times as naturally as breathing – but now it felt like the very first time: *Ease the string back, relax, breathe out...*

A sickening thud. Dark's music cut off.

Renn lost her nerve. Clutching her bow, she raced for her axe. Couldn't reach it, Dark and Naiginn were rolling and grunting, locked in combat. Dark struggled to his knees, blood streaming down his face. He flung Naiginn's knife down the slope, then his quiver, arrows clattering. Naiginn sprang to his feet, swinging his axe. Dark kicked his legs from under him. Naiginn fell with a crash, his axe flying over the edge. He was up before Renn could grab her weapon. Dark sank to his knees, toppled forwards and lay still.

Coughing, spitting blood, Naiginn tossed Renn's axe off the slab and wrenched his club from his belt. Hefting it, admiring its bear-tooth spikes, he lunged at her.

'What you're doing is mad!' shouted Renn, dodging another sweep of Naiginn's club as they circled each other around the slab. 'This Rite is our only chance! If the First Tree doesn't come back we're all going to die!'

'I'm a demon!' taunted Naiginn. 'I can't die!'

'You can when you're in a mortal body!'

He cackled. 'And in another instant I'll shed it like a broken husk! Once I've gouged out your eyes and ripped out your tongue, once I've eaten your souls – I'll be *free*! The First Tree won't *matter* any more! I'll devour every living soul in the Forest! I'll slaughter the sun itself!'

'I won't *let* you!' she yelled, throwing the contents of her medicine pouch in his face. 'Earthblood and mammut ash: what demons fear most!'

'I fear *nothing*,' he roared – but he was blinking, thrown off balance.

Seizing her chance, Renn scrambled up the rocks above the slab, seeking somewhere to shoot the four arrows before he cut her down.

Wolf saw the pack-sister fleeing the demon, but he could only reach them through a gap between unclimbable boulders, and the bear was in his way.

Wolf darted in and snapped at its heels. It swung round with a snarl, its massive forepaw missing Wolf's head by a whisker. He had to find another way.

The rocks were slippery with Bright Hard Cold, but he came to a place where they weren't so steep, heaved himself up. The demon had seen him and taken refuge on a boulder so high that Wolf couldn't reach. And to Wolf's horror, the pack-sister hadn't grabbed her chance and fled, instead she'd jumped back onto the flat rock where she stood, bracing her hind legs, aiming her Long-Claw-that-Flies at the Up.

And now the bear was coming after Wolf.

TWENTY-EIGHT

Deep in the bear's marrow, Torak battled to stop it attacking Wolf – but its souls were too strong, and with appalling speed it lunged at his pack-brother. Wolf dodged a heartbeat too late, one giant paw grazing his shoulder, sending him yelping through the air.

He landed with a thud, sprang to his feet, darted in for another attack – then retreated, taunting his foe. Bellowing with fury, the bear battered rocks, sending them bouncing down the slope. In its simple mind Torak felt its blood-hunger with horrifying force: it would snap Wolf's spine and grab his skull in its jaws, it would maul till there was nothing left but mangled meat...

No! roared Torak's spirit with a ferocity he hadn't known he possessed. *You shall not attack my pack-brother!*

Before the startled bear could raise a paw against Wolf, Torak wrenched it to his will. The bear spun round, and in two bounds attained the flat rock, just as Naiginn was leaping down and advancing on Renn.

With the bear's keen nose Torak smelt the ice demon's stink, its dark souls sealed in its prison of man-flesh. With lightning speed he attacked – but Naiginn was a skilled hunter, he knew where to strike, his spiked club dealing the bear an agonizing blow on its sensitive snout.

Outraged, it reared and flung its arms wide. It would crush the demon's skull like an egg, it would rip open its belly and feast on its guts... And its hunger to kill was Torak's own hunger to kill, a red mist engulfing his spirit. At last he was fighting the demon who had attacked his mate – but this time he was no captive, he had the strength of the mightiest hunter in the Forest.

With both forepaws he slashed at Naiginn – who dodged, warding him off with his club. Renn was forgotten, Naiginn's only thought was escape.

For an instant his eyes grazed the bear's – and his pale stare widened. 'I know you're in there, spirit walker!' he gasped. 'But I'm your bone kin, remember? Kill me and you're outcast for ever, you could never be with Renn again!'

The red mist had Torak in its power. He was not to be deterred, he would tear the demon limb from limb...

Suddenly music was piercing his dull bear's brain. A thin, supple stream of sound, shaky at first, yet gaining strength as it spiralled into the sky.

The bear faltered. Torak felt the red mist lift.

What happened next took only moments, but time stretched, so that he perceived it as if it lasted all night.

He saw Dark on his knees, blood streaming down his face as he played the mammut-bone flute.

He saw Renn standing with legs braced, shooting arrow after arrow at incredible speed, each arrowhead biting the tail of the one before as she sent them soaring towards the stars.

And with a pang Torak knew that it wasn't enough, because they were missing the final thing that would make the Rite complete:

The brightest souls in the Forest.

Wolf, scrambling onto the flat rock to save the pack-sister, heard the voice of the singing bone twisting high into the Up.

He saw the bear stand swaying – and he sensed that it wasn't attacking the pack-sister, it was *protecting* her.

The demon knew this too, it was fleeing downhill towards the dogs and the sliding tree. For an instant Wolf was tempted to give chase. But now the pack-sister was shooting her Long-Claws-that-Fly into the Up, so fast they were streaming in a shining arc – and at last Wolf understood why she'd abandoned Tall Tailless: *she was trying to bring back the Tree of Light.*

Her Long Claws weren't going to reach it, they couldn't fly high enough. Not on their own.

Then Wolf, with the strange certainty that came to him at times, put up his muzzle and howled. He howled as he had never howled before, sending howl after howl soaring far into the Up, carrying the pack-sister's Long Claws all the way through the Dark to the swaying, singing Tree of Light.

Tears stung Renn's eyes as Wolf's howls thrilled through her marrow. The brightest souls in the Forest were singing, and their song was as swift and strong as a mountain stream: it held the power of the Sea and the beauty of snow, the warmth of love and the teeming life of the Forest – all flowing together in a shining thread of purest sound, a singing rainbow spanning the darkness, carrying her arrows far beyond the stars.

She sank to her knees. Dark sagged against a rock, the mammut-bone flute forgotten in his hand.

As they listened, their eyes never left the sky, desperately searching for the faintest glimmer of green that would tell them the Rite had worked.

Still on its hind legs, the bear listened in puzzlement to the wolf's piercing song, and in its marrow Torak felt the last trace of blood-lust lift from his spirit, like a stain rinsed away by clear water.

Far below, he saw Naiginn on his sled whipping his dogs past a silent band of Chosen Ones who stood watching him go.

He felt the bear give a startled huff, and shake itself: *What's going on? How did I get here?*

Then, huffing and snorting, it dropped on all fours and ambled off towards the Forest.

TWENTY-NINE

Renn dreams it's summer in the sacred valley.

From the rockfall a new river is flowing, filling the hollow gouged by the Thunderstar to make a beautiful blue lake. Fish shimmer and dart in its waters, and around it are murmurous woods that shelter hunters and prey. Beside the lake a new sacred grove is burgeoning: young hollies encircle an oak sapling and a sturdy little yew. The Forest is healing itself. It is growing a fresh green heart...

Renn woke in a nest of warm fur. Somewhere nearby, a flock of siskins was twittering. Too drowsy to open her eyes, she lay listening, savouring the dream's afterglow.

Siskins? She opened her eyes. That must mean she was back in the unburnt Forest.

A fearsome face loomed over her: a shaven skull plastered with yellow clay, bark-like scars, two greeny-brown eyes smiling into hers.

Renn started up. 'Where's Torak! Dark? My bow? Are they all right?'

Gently the Auroch woman pushed her down. 'They're fine, you'll see them later. First you must eat.'

Her name was Aksash and she wouldn't take no for an answer, watching in respectful silence as Renn devoured a bowl of stew which contained lots of mushrooms and not enough squirrel.

While she ate, Renn tried to piece together what had happened after the Rite. She remembered staunching Dark's head wound with snow, then struggling with him down the rockfall.

To her astonishment she'd found Iakim and his band caring for Torak – or rather they were staring as he sat with his back against the wreck of the Great Yew, mumbling and casting about with unseeing eyes.

Renn had felt too drained to explain that he was spirit walking, but she hadn't needed to: having seen him escape with the sacred herd, the Chosen Ones no longer believed he was a Skin-Taker. As for her, they'd seen her perform the Rite; and Dark, with his cobwebby hair and white raven companion, had gained their instant respect.

Most important of all, they'd learnt the truth about Naiginn. He was not their Great Leader, he was an ice demon, who – far from wielding mastery over bears – had fled in terror from a real one. How *could* they have been so wrong?

After that Renn remembered little, except being carried down-valley on a litter...

She asked Aksash how long she'd been asleep.

'A long time,' said Aksash. 'We gave you a potion. You'd done great Magecraft, you needed much sleep.'

'I thought Chosen Ones hated Magecraft.'

The woman hung her head in shame. 'Not any more. And we're not Chosen Ones, we're back to being separate clans.'

Belatedly, Renn realized that Aksash wasn't covered in chalk. The rolls of alder bark in her ears were red, her clothes were brown reindeer fur, and the amulet on her breast was golden horn.

'But being back in your old clans is good, isn't it?' said Renn.

'You don't understand, we were tricked by a *demon*! We'll carry that burden for ever!' She lapsed into gloomy silence, and Renn gave up.

She found Dark outside, sitting by a fire. He was carving a small piece of green slate, watched by a gaggle of admiring children and dogs. His head had been deftly bandaged with wovenbark and he was so pale his skin was almost transparent, dark-blue shadows under his eyes.

He gave Renn a crooked smile. 'Torak's better. He's in the Forest with Wolf. Here's your bow, I've looked after it.'

As Renn checked it over, she decided not to tell him about her dream. She wasn't sure if she'd actually seen

242

those colours, or just imagined them afterwards – and this mattered, because only her coloured dreams came true.

It was peaceful, watching Dark carve. A woman shooed away the children and dogs, but one dog slunk back. Absently, Dark stroked its ear. The dog stiffened – then faintly wagged its tail. Renn guessed it had never been stroked.

Not far away, three women were scrubbing chalk off mounds of clothes with handfuls of snow.

'Strange people,' murmured Dark. 'They're determined to punish themselves for having believed in Naiginn.'

'What about the Skin-Takers?'

'Ah, that's different. I tried to explain, but they couldn't bring themselves to believe they were scared of creatures that didn't exist. In the end I told them Skin-Takers only attack if they've got eyes, and that I sent Ark to peck them out, so that was the end of the Skin-Takers. That they believe.'

Renn laughed.

They were silent, enjoying the warmth of the fire and the crisp winter sun.

Renn asked what Dark was making. He showed her. The little beaver was almost finished: sitting on its haunches, holding a tiny green egg in its paws; Dark had carved the egg from a leftover chip of heartstone. 'To help the Forest heal,' he said. 'I'm going to bury it at the sacred grove.'

Renn didn't want to think about that night. Or about Naiginn escaping down the valley…

Dark said quietly, 'They found his bearskin robes in the cave. They burnt them.'

'What about Naiginn himself?'

He shook his head. 'They tracked his sled to the Jaws of the Deep Forest, then lost the trail.' He paused. 'Realvi's gone too.'

'Oh, Dark.'

'Maybe he followed his Leader,' he said without expression. 'Or went back to the Mountains. I don't care.'

They both knew that wasn't true.

Renn said she was off to find Torak, and did Dark want to come? She was relieved when he said no, then felt bad in case he'd guessed and felt left out.

Both were sharply aware that she hadn't asked the one question she'd been burning to ask since she'd woken up. There was no point. If the First Tree had returned, Dark would have told her at once.

Aksash had cleaned and mended Renn's clothes and given her an under-jerkin and -leggings of fluffy white hare fur. She'd also re-soled Renn's boots and provided leaf-shaped snowshoes strung with sinew.

To say sorry for destroying her old bow, Tseid had given her a wovenbark quiver full of arrows fletched with black woodpecker feathers. Renn could see that they would shoot true.

The pines sparkled with hoarfrost as she followed Torak's tracks uphill. The only sounds were the creak of her snowshoes and the whump of snow falling from a branch.

She found Torak halfway up a spruce tree, so absorbed in taking honeycomb from a bees' nest that he didn't hear her approach. Bees were buzzing around his head, but smoke from the smouldering brand he'd stuck in a fork was making them too drowsy to sting.

Renn watched him place the honeycomb in a birch-bark basket slung over his shoulder. He wore a new parka and leggings of supple brown reindeer fur that caught the sun as he moved, and his face had lost its stretched look. Already the cut on his cheek was a long, clean scab: like a wolf, he healed quickly.

Sensing her presence, he called down to her, smiling on one side of his mouth so as not to crack his scab.

It was the first time they'd been alone since he'd been taken captive. Fast as a pine marten, he shinned down the trunk, threw off the basket and pulled her into his arms.

'Mind my bow!' she cried, laughing.

With exaggerated care he took her bow and quiver and hung them on a branch, then pulled her back into his arms. He smelt of woodsmoke and wolf, and she could taste that he'd been at the honey.

'The black web,' she said when she could breathe. 'It's gone, isn't it?'

'How can you tell?'

'Your eyes: the green flecks are back. I've missed them...
I've missed you.' She paused. 'That night, after the Rite.
You were talking, but not making any sense.'

'What was I saying?'

'You kept telling me to dig you up and plant you on
the slope. Eventually I worked out that you were spirit
walking in a yew seedling we found among some rocks.'

'Did you do it? Did you move the seedling?'

She nodded. 'Well, I got Iakim to do it. But why? You
seemed to think it was important.'

'I don't know, I don't remember anything about it.'

She shivered. 'I hate it when you spirit walk in trees. I'm
terrified you'll never come back. Don't ever do it again.'

Pushing a lock of her hair behind her ear, he kissed the
freckle at the corner of her mouth. 'I'll always come back.'

It wasn't the answer she wanted, but she let it go. She
knew there were things he wasn't telling her. And she
wondered whether, now that the black web was gone, he
could finally see green. But for the moment she would let
that go too. She wanted this time with him to be as it was
before the Thunderstar: the scent of winter on his skin, his
lean brown face smiling down at her.

He touched the scab on his cheekbone. 'I'll have quite
a scar. D'you mind?'

''Course not, it's part of you.'

They watched a black woodpecker pecking a pine cone
jammed in a tree-trunk. The bird saw them looking and
fled, tik-tikking in alarm.

'We need more honey,' said Torak.

Renn made him another torch with a wad of folded birch-bark and he climbed back up and took a second comb from the hole in the trunk, leaving two for the bees.

After that they both thanked the bees, then Torak broke off a piece of honeycomb and tucked it in a fork as an offering to the Forest, and Renn left some for her clan guardians. Rip and Rek were playing at rolling down a snowdrift, landing in a heap at the bottom, then flying uphill to do it again.

Torak left a bigger chunk at the foot of another spruce, in case the bear was still around. 'It'll be hungry if it hasn't yet found a new Den.'

Renn was surprised. 'Does that mean you've made your peace with bears? What's changed?'

He hesitated. 'Tell you later. But I think that now when I remember Fa, it won't be as he was that last night. It'll be as he was before.'

They munched honeycomb, Renn sucking every drop of delirious sweetness and spitting out the wax to put in her medicine pouch, Torak swallowing the lot, as he always did.

Dusk was settling on the Forest, but Renn couldn't sense any demons. The ravens shook the snow from their feathers and flew off to roost. In the distance Wolf howled.

Before Torak could howl back, another wolf answered. Torak raised his eyebrows. 'Sounds like a stranger wolf who's lost his pack. I wonder what that's about.' But as

Wolf didn't seem worried, Torak decided to leave him to sort it out on his own.

They didn't feel like returning to camp, so they scooped a hollow in a snowdrift and snuggled together, watching the stars come out and the sky turn from pale gold to luminous violet to deepest blue.

The new Willow Grouse Moon wouldn't rise until much later. Renn followed the great swathe of stars that arched across the sky: the trail of First Raven's snowshoes after he'd stolen the sun.

But no First Tree, she thought with a stab of worry.

Torak's arm tightened around her. 'When you did the Rite... I've never seen anyone shoot like that. You were amazing.'

She squirmed. 'I hated leaving you in the snow. You do know that?'

'Renn. No one could have shot better than you.'

'What does that matter, if...' She broke off. Neither of them wanted to voice what they were thinking.

What if the Rite hadn't worked?

THIRTY

Fin-Kedinn asked Torak to go with him into the Dead Lands, taking scoop-nets and birch-bark pails.

'Why can't we go ice fishing nearer camp?' protested Torak.

'Because,' said his foster father.

While Torak and Renn had been away, Guvach of the Red Deer had journeyed to Crowwater and told Fin-Kedinn about the unburnt Forest south of the Shield. The clans were now camped by the Blackwater, in the Open Forest west of the Jaws. This had made it easy for Iakim's dog sleds to take Torak, Renn and Dark downriver to join them.

But why, Torak wondered, do we have to trudge back to the Dead Lands to go fishing?

Four days into the Willow Grouse Moon, and still no First Tree. The Chosen Ones – as he continued to think of them – had returned his wolf amulet, wrist-guard and medicine horn, and given him a new axe and knife of green basalt; but to him both weapons looked grey. He hadn't told Renn that he still couldn't see green, but she'd guessed. Did this mean the Rite had failed and the First Tree was never coming back?

When he'd tried asking Wolf, his pack-brother had simply replied that he couldn't hear the Tree of Light. And Torak couldn't ask if it would come, because in wolf talk there is no future.

'Here,' said Fin-Kedinn.

They'd reached the banks of a frozen river, a dismal place in the half-light of dawn: wet snow falling, dripping skeletons of trees. Fin-Kedinn's dog Grip stood with drooping ear and tail. His master was already at work.

When the Thunderstar struck, a landslip had cut off a small lake a few paces upstream. Fin-Kedinn stood on the river ice just below the landslip, hacking a hole with his axe. Reluctantly, Torak helped. When it was done, Fin-Kedinn climbed past the landslip to the lake and started hacking a bigger hole.

Torak stayed where he was. He thought of all the clans who'd been lost to the Thunderstar: the Lynxes, the Boars, the Otters. All the dead trees, all the creatures... He flung down his axe. 'Why did this happen?' he shouted. 'Why?'

'I don't know,' said Fin-Kedinn without stopping work. 'But how does anger help?'

'Is that all you can say?'

'D'you want me to pretend I have the answer?'

Torak glared at him. 'Is that it? We don't know why it happened, so we just carry on?'

'Nothing else we can do.' Putting his hand to the old wound on his thigh, Fin-Kedinn straightened up. 'This was a good lake before the Thunderstar. It fed big shoals of young bream.'

Torak did not reply. He watched his foster father fill his pail with lake water and set it down. Next Fin-Kedinn stuck his scoop-net into the ice hole, then yanked it out and flicked a wriggling silver breamling into the pail. The fish was too small to be worth eating, but in another three summers it might feed many people. Trapped in what was left of the lake, it would never get the chance.

Moodily, Torak watched Fin-Kedinn limp downhill and empty his pail into the hole in the river ice – where, if it was lucky, the breamling might get to grow up.

'But what's the point?' cried Torak. 'Must be thousands of them trapped in this lake, what difference will you make by saving a single fish?'

'I made a difference to that one,' said Fin-Kedinn. 'Are you going to help, or just stand there?'

Glowering, Torak picked up his net.

The breamlings didn't want to be netted, and he became absorbed in catching them. When his net got snagged with Fin-Kedinn's they paused to untangle them, and Torak was astonished to find that it was nearly dusk.

Fin-Kedinn was watching him, his blue eyes smiling.

Torak broke into a wry grin. 'I think we've saved a few hundred,' he muttered.

'At least,' agreed his foster father.

Torak felt a surge of love for him: for being wiser, braver and kinder than anyone he knew.

As they headed back to the Blackwater, Fin-Kedinn told Torak that tomorrow they would break camp and head north to the Widewater.

Torak looked at him. 'But that's even further into the Dead Lands. Why camp there?'

Fin-Kedinn's hard features gave nothing away. 'You don't remember. Let's just say there's something we need to do.'

ᚵ ᚵ

'We can't do this,' cried Sialot. 'It's not possible!'

Murmurs of agreement from the crowd.

Renn, standing on the riverbank with Torak and Dark, thought so too. She kept quiet out of loyalty to her uncle.

They'd broken camp and after a long trudge had reached the Widewater. But instead of the greatest river in the Forest, what they saw was a dismal mountain of tumbled rocks and splintered trees.

Belatedly, Renn remembered the scouts' reports after

the Thunderstar struck: 'Half the Hogback's collapsed, it's buried the Widewater... If the river's not flowing by spring, the salmon won't come...'

Now she understood why Fin-Kedinn hadn't taken this route when he'd led the clans south to the Blackwater. He hadn't wanted them to face this appalling sight, not till they were strong enough to take it. Judging by their faces, they still weren't.

Renn watched him climb the 'mountain' of debris, leaning on his staff, with Grip at his heels. He turned to address the clans. 'We can do this,' he said in a carrying voice. 'We can clear all this away! The river will run again – *if* we work together!'

'No, we can't!' protested Gaup of the Salmon Clan. 'Face it, Fin-Kedinn, it's too big!'

'The Widewater will never run again!' declared Durrain of the Red Deer. 'And if the Widewater's blocked, the salmon won't return to the other rivers either! It's the will of the World Spirit, there's nothing we can do!'

'I don't believe that,' retorted Fin-Kedinn. 'This river has always been good to us, now it needs our help.'

He scanned the clans who'd followed him into the Dead Lands, and the people of the Deep Forest who'd answered his call. 'Every one of you knows our ancestors' story: how all the creatures came together and survived the Great Wave. Well, we're going to make a new story: how the clans moved the mountain and saved the river! Who's with me?'

People looked at each other, hung their heads. No one looked at Fin-Kedinn.

'I am!' cried Torak, Renn and Dark together.

'Me too!' cried Sialot, surprising them.

'And me!' shouted Guvach with a glance at Durrain.

'The Bat Clan is with you!' called Iakim, who'd been chosen as its new Leader.

And so began the greatest task the clans had ever attempted. Everyone agreed that Fin-Kedinn must be in charge, and he swiftly ensured that while they all did their share of digging away at the 'mountain', each clan would also perform those additional tasks which suited them best.

Thus the Willows gathered bark, which the Rowans and Bats made into baskets and ropes for hauling earth. The Red Deer and Ravens kept everyone fed by hunting; the Whales, Salmon and Kelp by ice fishing; the Rowans and Vipers fed the fires; and the Deep Forest clans happily punished themselves by gutting fish and digging dungpits. As for cooking, when fights broke out over who refused to eat what, the Sea-eagles simply mixed all the supplies together to make delicious stews – which pleased everyone, because by then they were too exhausted to care.

Fin-Kedinn was tireless: advising, lending a hand, sounding the shift changes on his birch-bark horn. At first Durrain kept apart, but Dark persuaded her, and soon she was busy tending sprains and broken bones.

Even the dogs helped, dragging sleds laden with logs, carrying saddle-packs to the dumping grounds. And one day the Walker strode into camp, and revealed an unexpected skill at levering boulders without causing further landslips.

It was grindingly hard work, and as the Willow Grouse Moon wore on, spirits flagged. They revived when word came that the Mountain Hare Clan had survived the Thunderstar, as well as the Wolf Clan in the south.

Then, without warning, the Otter Clan appeared. It turned out that their Mages had foreseen the cliff-fall that would drown their shelters, so they'd fled to the far shore of Lake Axehead before the Thunderstar struck. They set to work with a will, and as they were superlative fishermen, everyone was soon enjoying piles of eel and pike, which made a welcome change. (The Walker, who was an outcast from the Otter Clan, had quietly vanished.)

Torak and Renn hardly saw each other. Torak was hauling boulders all day, Renn was busy filling baskets of earth, carrying them Kelp-fashion on her back with a strap across her forehead. When their shifts ended they piled together like wolf cubs and fell instantly asleep.

Fin-Kedinn had set two teams digging a channel through the 'mountain' from either end, and a day finally came when they met in the middle. Ragged cheers went up as muddy river water began to flow. It would freeze overnight, but nobody cared. When spring came and the

Widewater thawed, it would widen the channel by itself –
and soon after that the salmon would return.

If, thought Renn, the First Tree ever comes back.

They'd finished nightmeal and as she was too tired to
go inside, she sat slumped against Torak, staring owlishly
at the fire.

Dark gave a huge yawn and fed another worm to Spike
the hedgehog. Dark's head wound had healed, but his eyes
were still shadowed. He'd told Renn that ghosts still
thronged the Forest. Without the First Tree they had
nowhere to go.

Torak, running a lock of Renn's hair through his fingers,
was staring up at the stars. 'And still it doesn't come.'

In a few days it would be the Moon of Green Snow,
when the First Tree used to shine brightest: sometimes so
bright that it turned the snow green...

'If it doesn't we're finished,' said Renn. 'All this will have
been for nothing.'

'That's why Fin-Kedinn's been working us so hard,' said
Dark. 'Keeps our minds off it.'

'It hasn't been for nothing,' Torak said quietly.

Renn twisted round and looked at him.

It was beginning to snow, speckling his shoulders, his
dark hair. 'Look what we've done,' he said. 'Clans working
together, never giving up. No, Renn, I'm with Fin-Kedinn.
Whatever happens, this hasn't been for nothing.'

Wolf trotted to the edge of his range, where the two stranger wolves waited at a respectful distance. Wolf halted, hackles bristling, head and tail stiffly raised. Coldly he stared past the strangers.

Darkfur and Pebble stood a few paces behind him, waiting to see what he would do. Either he would let the strangers join the pack, or chase them away – or he, Darkfur and Pebble would kill them.

With pleading whines the newcomers slunk towards him, dropping their ears, clamping their tails between legs. *We lost our pack to the Great Bright Beast from the Up. Can we join yours?*

Wolf smelt that they were brother and sister, barely full-grown. Terrified. The brother was stocky, with a white muzzle and throat. The sister had one black ear, one grey. She was smaller but cleverer, Wolf could tell from her eyes.

Braver too. Politely averting her gaze, she belly-crawled towards him and tried to lick his muzzle. He raised his head so that her tongue only brushed his neck.

Her brother approached and they rolled onto their backs, whimpering, waggling their paws: *Can we join?*

Wolf sniffed their breath, then under their tails. The female would be a fast runner, useful in the chase. Her brother could help bring down the kill. Both could guard the range and watch over new cubs.

Briefly Wolf met his mate's eyes. With a twitch of his ears he walked back to her and Pebble, leaving the young wolves to follow. Good. It was decided. Two new wolves in the pack.

Later Tall Tailless came, and agreed that this was good. He was pack-leader, so he decided most things, but it was right that Wolf had decided this.

At Tall Tailless's approach, Whitethroat and Blackear had fled; but Wolf and Darkfur had soon brought them back, and with Tall Tailless's help the young wolves were beginning to understand that they'd joined a pack like no other.

Wolf was happy. The pack was bigger and stronger: earlier they'd killed a reindeer. He'd eaten his fill and Darkfur and Pebble were still at the carcass, Pebble quietly growling to remind the new wolves to wait their turn.

Whitethroat was hiding a pigeon carcass he'd found in the Bright Soft Cold. His sister Blackear was pretending not to notice, so that she could steal it when he wasn't looking. The ravens perched in a pine, on the lookout for scraps.

Tall Tailless knelt and put his forehead against Wolf's. *Your Breath-that-Walks*, he said. *It's very very bright.*

Wolf licked his ear. *And you're better. The black roots are gone.*
Yes.
But you still smell of bear.
Sorry.

Together they sat listening to the trees talking to each other, and strong wolf jaws crunching bones.

Tall Tailless said something about the pale-pelted demon that Wolf didn't understand, so he told his pack-brother that the pale-pelted demon was far away. Tall Tailless said maybe, but he was still a danger. Wolf said he could defend the pack from the demon: this was what Wolf was for.

His mate and Pebble had stopped eating and were having fun sliding about on the frozen Fast Wet.

Wolf sprang to his feet and went down on his forepaws before his pack-brother, lashing his tail: *Come on, let's play!*

'Fin-Kedinn wants you in the shelter,' Gaup called to Renn.

'What about?' she said, skating to the riverbank and grabbing a branch to steady herself.

'Two scouts have arrived, that's all I know.' A gaggle of whooping children claimed him; he chuckled as they dragged him away.

Fin-Kedinn had declared a three-day feast to celebrate freeing the Widewater, and everything was uproariously upside down. People were wearing their clothes inside out, dogs were allowed inside shelters, children ordered grown-ups about. A hollowed-out log had been filled with fish for the dead, and anyone with mourning marks had washed them off.

For a time, grief and worry over the First Tree were set aside. In their place was dancing, eating too much, and holding skating races on the river. Shamik, unstoppable on her shinbone skates, won every time.

Renn liked skating, but she missed Torak and Dark. Dark had left days before to bury his slate beaver at the sacred grove. Torak was on the Hogback with Wolf.

She found Fin-Kedinn in the Ravens' shelter with a man and a girl she didn't know. Both had the sharp brown features of the Otter Clan, and were blowing on beakers of pine-needle brew which Halut had made. Both were staring at the Kelp woman's bizarrely narrow head.

Firelight leapt in Fin-Kedinn's eyes as he motioned to Renn to sit. 'They found Naiginn's sled,' he told her.

Her spirits plunged. 'Not Naiginn himself?'

He shook his head.

The Otter girl said: 'He'd left his dogs tied up. Starving, terrified.'

'We lost his tracks at the northernmost edge of the Forest,' said the man. 'Heading onto the fells.'

Renn frowned. 'That could be a trick. He could've doubled back.'

Fin-Kedinn nodded. 'I've spoken to the other clan Leaders. They know what he is and what he looks like. He won't get near you or Torak.'

She did not reply. In the distance Torak was howling with the wolves. They sounded happy. She wished Torak was down here, where he'd be safe.

'The wolves have strong voices,' said Halut, baring her fangs in a smile.

'But what does the demon *want?*' said the Otter girl.

'Souls,' said Renn. 'He wants to break free of the spell trapping him in his mortal body. He thinks if he—' She broke off. She'd just had a dreadful thought. On the night of the Rite, Wolf's howls had sped her arrows on their way: *Wolf*, who had the brightest souls in the Forest... And Naiginn had heard him.

'Renn?' said Fin-Kedinn. 'What's wrong?'

She made to reply – but at that moment Dark burst in.

Breathless and excited, he hadn't stopped to brush snow off his clothes. 'I was watching the sky! Suddenly I heard a humming all around, then I saw—'

'Saw what?' said Fin-Kedinn.

Dark was beaming. 'Ghosts rising into the sky! So many, and all at peace, going where they'll find shelter!'

Renn and Fin-Kedinn exchanged glances. To Dark she said: 'D'you think that means—'

'Come and see!' Seizing her wrist, he pulled her outside.

People were falling to their knees, laughing, crying, reaching for the sky.

Renn's eyes began to sting. Craning her neck, she gazed at the vast boughs of luminous green that were shimmering and rippling across the stars. The First Tree was shining its miraculous light upon the Forest.

Torak came running down from the Hogback, grinning from ear to ear.

'Can you see the green?' she cried.

'*I can see it!*' he shouted.

And now they were laughing and whirling round and round, showering each other with handfuls of beautiful, glittering green snow.

AUTHOR'S NOTE

The world of Torak and Renn is that of six thousand years ago. That's after the Ice Age, but before farming spread to Scandinavia – when the land was one vast forest.

The people looked like you or me, but they were hunter-gatherers. They lived in small clans, some staying at a campsite for a few days or moons, others staying put all year round. They didn't have writing, metals or the wheel – but they didn't need them. They were superb survivors. They knew all about the animals, trees, plants and rocks on which they survived. When they wanted something they knew where to find it, or how to make it.

Like the previous books in the series, *Skin Taker* takes place in northern Scandinavia, so the wildlife is appropriate to the region – as are the seasonal changes in the hours of daylight. However I've changed mountains, rivers and coastlines to suit the stories, which means that you won't find the specific features of Torak's world in a modern atlas.

I got the idea for a meteorite hitting the Forest about five years ago, when I was starting to think about the three books which would become *Viper's Daughter*, *Skin Taker* and the forthcoming *Wolfbane*. I wanted to write about the effect of a worldwide disaster on Torak and his people. I had no idea that by the time I finished writing *Skin Taker*, most of the world would be in lockdown, battling the threat of Covid-19.

To gain insights into how Torak's people perceive the meteorite strike, I've studied eyewitness accounts of the Evenk people of the remote Tunguska region of Siberia, which was famously blasted by a meteorite in 1908. These reindeer herders' accounts were written down decades later, but they retain the freshness of indelible memories.

I've often been in the Arctic during the winter darkness, but for *Skin Taker* I reminded myself of what it's like by visiting Kirkenes in the far north of Norway in January 2020. I then travelled by Hurtigruten down the coast of Norway to Bergen (little knowing that within weeks this would be impossible, thanks to the coronavirus). Apart from immersing myself in a world of snow, ice and false dawns, I took a starlit ride on the shaggiest Icelandic horse I've ever seen, and from the ship's top deck I saw the First Tree several times, including on one memorable night when a meteor shot across the sky behind its shimmering green lights.

My 2016 research trip to Haida Gwaii in British Columbia and to Alaska gave me all sorts of inspiration for the story. Naiginn's bear-clawed gauntlets are based on the shamanic regalia of one of the First Nations of the Pacific Northwest, and his bear-claw circlet is based on that of a Tlingit shaman. The Kelp Clan's narrow heads were inspired by the traditional practices of the Kwakwaka'wakw (formerly Kwakiutl) and Coast Salish people. A young Inupiaq man in Alaska told me about the bear trap formed from a spiked strip of baleen, which Naiginn uses to lethal effect. (I read somewhere that the Sami traditionally used something similar to kill wolves.) More benignly, the young man also described times when he's out on the winter tundra and the Northern Lights shine so brightly they turn the snow green.

Bushwhacking trips in the rainforests of Alaska, notably on Baranof Island, furnished me with details for Torak's bear-tracking – although luckily (and unlike Torak), my companions and I didn't come across a bear kill. I did, though, crawl into a grizzly bear's den, complete with two side-chambers for the cubs. Of course the grizzly wasn't home, but fresh tracks, piles of dung and scratch-marks on tree-trunks told us it wasn't far off. That lent an interesting flavour to our hike.

Still on bears, the episode when Torak bumps into a bear on a foggy river is based on the experience of an intrepid young Norwegian hiker whom I met on a trip to Malangenfjord in 2015. The same young woman also told me of a separate incident when she'd scared off a bear from entering her tent with a puff of pepper spray; I substituted earthblood when this happens to Dark.

Concerning caves, I've been down lots of them for previous stories in the series, and each one has given me fresh ideas. For Dark's forays underground in *Skin Taker* I spent an unforgettable day down Clearwell Caves in the Royal Forest of Dean, Gloucestershire. The caves have been mined for over four thousand years for iron and ochre (that's the soft mineral ferric oxide – or earthblood, as the clans call it). I was lucky enough to be guided by Jonathan Wright, who runs the caves, and whose family have been freeminers for centuries. In addition to the beautiful and sensitively presented show caves, Jonathan took me into the Deep Levels of Old Ham Mine, to a depth of about two hundred feet, all of which gave me ideas for the story too numerous to mention. Highlights included seeing (and clawing at) veins of red, yellow and purple ochre in situ in the cave walls; drinking astonishingly pure water from a flowstone pool; and learning of the miners' clever traditional light-holder, or 'Nelly', made from a stick and a ball of clay. I also experienced the disorientation of utter darkness and silence deep underground; and I belly-crawled through a tunnel so impossibly small that I only plucked up the courage to go in because Jonathan had gone before me and I'd have been ashamed not to give it a try.

As for wolves, I was a patron of the UK Wolf Conservation Trust since *Wolf Brother* came out in 2004 until it closed to the public and the wolves went into well-deserved retirement in 2018. The wolves' different characters continue to provide inspiration for the stories.

Now I need to thank some people, including the crews and guides of: the Island Roamer, on which I explored Haida Gwaii, and the Wilderness Adventurer, on which I spent time in Alaska's Inside Passage and Glacier Bay National Park, both in 2016; and the MS Spitsbergen of the Hurtigruten Line, on my trip from Kirkenes to Bergen in January 2020.

My particular thanks go to Jonathan Wright of Clearwell Caves, for so generously giving up his entire day to take me down the caves, and for sharing fascinating stories from his decades-long experience of life underground.

I also want to thank Geoff Taylor for his magnificent chapter illustrations and the endpaper map, and John Fordham for his stunningly evocative cover design; as well as the diligent and enthusiastic staff of my publishers, Head of Zeus, for all their hard work in bringing out *Skin Taker* (and *Viper's Daughter* before it) under such exceptionally difficult conditions. As ever, very special thanks go to my agent Peter Cox, for his inexhaustible optimism and support and his imaginative ideas; and I am deeply grateful to Fiona Kennedy, my enormously talented editor and publisher, without whose enthusiasm and encouragement I would not have written these books.

Michelle Paver,
London 2021

michellepaver.com
wolfbrother.com

Torak, Renn and Wolf's final adventure

is out in April 2022.

Read the first chapter here.

ONE

The wolves have no idea that the Demon is watching. No idea that their shiny little lives could be snuffed out in a heartbeat.

Since dawn the Demon has been observing them from the ridge. Through the snowbound pines it makes out the red boulders where the she-wolf is digging her den. She's inside. Two wolves are padding about among the rocks. They seem to be guarding her, but they're bored and eager to play. One snaps an icicle off a boulder and bounds away, the other gives chase.

Now the she-wolf is backing out of the den. Her black pelt is clotted with mud, her belly swollen with unborn cubs. Hungrily the Demon licks the tang of her spirit off the wind. It would be easy to kill her, a single arrow destroying many lives... But she is not the one the Demon wants. The Demon is after her mate.

There.

Far up-valley near the frozen river, two more wolves are weaving between the trees. The lesser one with the white throat doesn't count; the Demon's quarry is the great grey wolf. Such souls it has, unbearably bright! The Demon hates and hungers for those souls – it longs to devour them and gain their power. Then at last it will claw its way out of this mortal body and be free...

Prickling with desire, the Demon pushes off on its long bone skates and sweeps downhill. It finds a snowbound thicket within arrowshot and downwind of the den. The she-wolf has gone back inside. Her "guardians" play on, oblivious.

The Demon takes an arrow from its quiver and sniffs the poison on its black flint head. It nocks the arrow to its bow.

Sooner or later, her mate will return. Yes.

The Demon settles to wait.

In the next valley to the south, Renn, studying the tracks Torak had found, caught a shiver of malice on the wind and lifted her head.

'What's wrong?' said Torak with his eyes on the snow.

'Not sure. Maybe just a trace of his presence.'

'But only a trace,' he said in disgust. 'If this *is* his trail it's two days old.'

In the distance Wolf howled. Torak cupped his hands to his mouth and howled back. An instant later they heard Wolf's deep-throated reply.

Renn threw Torak a questioning look. He shrugged. 'Whitethroat went after another beaver.'

'Are they allright?'

'Yes. Why?' He was walking slowly with his head down, his lean brown face remote as he scanned the snow for signs.

Renn didn't reply. Nine days into the Moon of Roaring

274

Rivers, and by now every valley should be noisy with cracking, grinding ice – and yet the thaw hadn't come. Winter still held the Forest in its grip. Was this why she felt a creeping unease?

Rip flew onto an overhead branch, scattering her with snow. 'I wish you wouldn't do that,' she muttered, brushing off her reindeer-hide parka. The raven fluffed his chin-feathers and gave her a gurgling greeting, then flew off, scattering more snow.

It's probably just lack of sleep, Renn told herself. Yesterday while making arrowheads she'd nicked the ball of her thumb, and the cut was swollen and painful. Last night's storm hadn't helped either. It was well out to Sea, nowhere near their camp, but since the Thunderstar struck, the most distant growl of thunder was enough to jolt her awake in a cold sweat.

Three moons since the disaster, and although the Burnt Lands were further east, even here by the coast the Forest bore scars: earlier they'd passed a swathe of pines felled by an earthshake.

Torak was beckoning to her and she hurried towards him, her snowshoes whispering over drifts.

He'd found a bootprint, boldly stamped for all to see.

'It's him, isn't it?' she said.

He nodded. 'Left foot turns slightly inwards. And I found this snagged on a branch.' Between finger and thumb he held up three long strands of yellow hair.

'Naiginn,' Renn said between her teeth.

Torak made to cast away the hairs but she took them from him. 'I may have a use for them.'

'A finding charm?'

'Maybe.'

'What's that over there?' he said in an altered voice.

Ten paces off, a young birch tree was dying. Its white bark had been wantonly slashed, and whoever had attacked it had made sure it would die by slicing away the soft bast underneath.

'Only a demon kills without reason,' growled Torak.

Nearby in the snow they found the body of an otter. Naiginn had eaten its eyes, tongue and brain, and had left the rest to rot, violating the Pact which forbade wasting any part of a kill.

A muscle worked in Torak's jaw. 'Scrabble marks in the snow. As if – oh no, she can't have been alive when...'

Renn felt sick with revulsion – and *shame*. Naiginn was her half-brother, her bone kin: an ice demon trapped in the body of a young man.

She pictured his once-handsome face, one side now puckered and scorched. His ice-blue eyes with their lightless black pupils. No human feeling, no sense of right or wrong.

Dead meat only gives me the taste of souls, he'd told Torak once. *I need living flesh! Every frightened, fluttering spirit makes me stronger – it loosens my bonds!*

Slipping off her mittens, Renn wrapped Naiginn's coiled hairs in a scrap of bast from the murdered birch and stowed them in her medicine pouch. While Torak laid his palm on the tree-trunk and quietly asked the Forest to help its souls find a new home, she stroked the otter's rich fur and bade its spirit be at peace. But was that possible if Naiginn had eaten its souls?

'Can you sense him at all?' Torak asked in a low voice.

She shook her head. Pushing back the sleeves of her parka, she showed him the zigzag tattoos on her wrists. 'They're not itching. He's long gone.' She frowned. She had a nagging sense that there was something they were missing.

Torak seemed to think so too. 'The last we heard of him,' he said thoughtfully, 'was the start of the Moon of Green Snow. Since then we've found no trace – until now. What was he doing *here*?'

'What do you mean?'

'Well, this part of the Forest's hardly deserted. The Willow Clan's camped just round that spur. Sea-eagles in the next valley, near the mouth of the Elk River, Ravens Clan upstream from them, then us and the wolves. And he knows we're after him, he knows the clans are on the lookout – so why is he blatantly *here*?'

'He's bad at hiding? He's from the Far North, doesn't know the Forest as we do.'

'But he knows enough to cover his tracks. Think about it, Renn. Three days ago he just *happened* to meet those Whale Clan fishermen out at the herring grounds – and "let slip" that he was heading here, to the Windriver?"

277

'He did give them a false name–'

'– but didn't bother hiding his clan-tattoos! I think he wanted them to suspect that he wasn't who he said. He knew they'd tell Fin-Kedinn – and that we'd get to hear of it. And now he's left this trail for us to find... No, Renn, he's telling us "Naiginn was here!"'

'Maybe he's daring us to come after him.'

'Mm.' Uneasily he fingered the green basalt axe jammed in his belt. 'He's after souls,' he mused, 'the brighter the better. So why bother with saplings?'

Suddenly Renn had a dreadful thought. Naiginn hungered for bright, strong souls – and one creature had the brightest of all. 'He's not after trees,' she said. 'This is a decoy.'

Torak's grey eyes widened and the blood drained from his face. 'He isn't luring us *to* him, he's luring us *away!*'

'Because he's not after us–'

'He's after Wolf.'

The reindeer threw down its head and charged at Wolf, who dodged its head-branches and darted round to nip its heels. Whitethroat, his less experienced pack-brother, leapt straight at its chest. The reindeer attacked with both forelegs, kicking Whitethroat nose over tail into a drift – then fled through the trees and galloped off along the frozen Fast Wet.

Whitethroat scrambled out of the drift and made to give chase, but Wolf shot him a glance: *Let it go!* The reindeer was too healthy and strong, not worth risking a spike in the guts.

Embarrassed, Whitethroat nuzzled under Wolf's chin to say sorry for spoiling the hunt, and Wolf gave him a reassuring soft-bite on the ear. *You learn. We go on.* Together they trotted up the slope to catch the smells.

The Hot Bright Eye was rising in the Up, and magpies were clattering about in the pines, snapping twigs for their nests. Wolf liked the time of the Bright Soft Cold, as the drifts made it easier to trap prey. And all was well with the pack. Tall Tailless and the pack-sister were hunting in the next valley, and Pebble and Blackear were guarding the Den. Darkfur was in a bad mood. She always was when her belly was full of cubs, but Wolf knew that if he tried to help her dig she would only growl at him and kick out furious spurts of earth.

The wind carried the scent of beaver: Whitethroat was eagerly sniffing. He was a fast runner, but young and not very clever. He still hadn't learnt that if you tried to dig a beaver from under the Bright Hard Cold, it simply swam away.

Suddenly Wolf caught a new scent that made his claws tighten and his hackles bristle. *Demon.*

Wolf knew in a snap that this wasn't one of the lesser demons that lurk in shadows and can be swiftly chased underground. This demon was cunning and immensely powerful. It stalked the Forest as a pale-pelted tailless, and in the past it had attacked Wolf and Tall Tailless and the pack-sister.

And this time it was horribly near the Den.

Q&A with Michelle Paver

How long did it take to write _Skin Taker_?

It took me the best part of a year. That might sound a lot, given that readers often tell me it only takes them a day or so to read the story – but as someone once said, '_Easy reading is very hard writing_'! That's certainly true for me. Once I had the idea of a catastrophe devastating the Forest, I did months of planning and research, including a trip to Alaska and Haida Gwaii (as described in the Author's Note). After that came my least favourite bit: writing the story from scratch. That took several months. Then I spent more months doing re-write after re-write. I much prefer that, though, because at least I've got something to work on, rather than having to face the awfulness of the blank page.

Only when I'm completely happy with a story do I send it to my marvellous publisher and editor, Fiona Kennedy, who has lived and breathed these books since _Wolf Brother_. Editing only takes a few weeks, and as there's never anything structural that needs doing, I quite enjoy it. The final stages involve a bit of buffing and polishing by copy-editors and proof-readers; but I'm incredibly fussy, and no one is allowed to change so much as a comma without my permission!

What are the joys and difficulties of writing a new story in such a well-loved series?

What I've enjoyed most is being back in the Forest with Torak, Renn and Wolf – not to mention Fin-Kedinn, Dark and the Walker. It's been fun seeing how they've developed after what they've been through in previous books. And writing the sequels has given me the chance to bring out aspects of the characters I didn't have time for before, such as Torak's attitude towards bears in *Skin Taker*. That's been very satisfying, and I hope it's something readers will enjoy too.

The trickiest thing has been ensuring that each new story appeals as a standalone adventure to readers who are new to Torak's world, while satisfying the fans' desire to know more about the characters whom they've come to regard as friends. I think I've succeeded – although obviously, that's for readers to judge.

You wrote much of *Skin Taker* during the pandemic. How did this affect things?

As I've worked from home for the last twenty years, I didn't expect to be all that affected – but I was wrong. I found that what was happening in the real world made it much harder to concentrate on writing. Also, as my sister and I had to become house-cleaner and gardener for our 90-year-old mother, I was constantly switching between the Stone Age Forest and more domestic concerns.

There was, though, one big silver lining: when Ian McKellen recorded the *Skin Taker* audiobook. At the beginning of the pandemic, I simply assumed that Ian wouldn't want to go anywhere near a recording studio, so I didn't even send him a proof copy of the book, as I usually do. I was astonished and delighted when he said that he was happy to do it, as he'd had both his Covid jabs. The recording took place under Covid-safe conditions, which meant that only Ian and the producer, Dylan, were in the studio. I was at home, holed up in my spare room, following every word on Skype, so that I could give Ian any support or information he needed. It was an unforgettable three days of eight-hour Skype sessions, and Ian's reading was truly magnificent. When he read the climax of the story, both Dylan and I were punching the air!

How does your research feed into the stories?

Like its predecessors, *Skin Taker* is first and foremost an adventure, and I do the research to make readers feel they're living the adventure with Torak, Renn and Wolf. That said, research is also great for giving me ideas for the stories, as I've mentioned in the Author's Note.

As regards creating Torak's world, over the years I've done a fair amount of archaeological research into the Stone Age, but for the clans' customs and beliefs, I've studied and talked to people who still live in traditional ways: including the Sami in northern Scandinavia, the Inuit in the Arctic, the Chukchi in Siberia, and the First Nations of the Pacific Northwest. Obviously what I've learnt from them aren't 'facts' about the Stone Age, but they've helped me create what I hope is an authentic-seeming Mesolithic world. And I've been pleased to find that the books have found favour with archaeologists.

Having said all this, only a tiny fraction of my research ever finds its way into the finished story, and I'm constantly having to resist the urge to 'get in' my favourite bits. For instance, when I was in the Alaskan rainforest I discovered a traditional First Nations cure for toothache: you lick a particular kind of very large, yellow-and-black slug. To find out if this worked, I duly licked a banana slug; there were lots of them lying about in the tangled forest where we were hiking. It worked, numbing my mouth for several minutes. But sadly, there turned out to be no place for this in either *Viper's Daughter* or *Skin Taker* – so I licked that slug in vain. (And just so you know, the slug was unharmed, and I laid it carefully back in the moss where I'd found it.)

㇓ ㇓

The maps at the front of the book are beautiful, as are the pictures at the start of each chapter. How do these come about?

I always do sketch-maps while I'm writing a story, so that I can track where the characters are, and make sure it all makes sense. While I'm writing, this sketch gets heavily scribbled on, as I often need to rearrange rivers and hills, and sometimes re-locate Torak and Renn, to fit the story. Once I've written the book, I tidy up the sketch of my now almost-illegible map, and send it to Geoff Taylor, the wonderful artist who has worked on the series since *Wolf Brother*. Geoff then creates a proper, beautiful map, with evocative border illustrations and a gorgeous compass. I always look forward to seeing what he comes up with, as he makes every map utterly distinct, and somehow manages to capture the flavour of each story.

The same goes for his chapter illustrations. Once I've finished the book, I send Geoff a note giving him a few alternative ideas for each chapter, so that he doesn't have to read the entire draft. I also give him information on any particular artefacts which feature in the story – such as the halibut hook in *Viper's Daughter* – and the various animals and plants. As with the maps, it's a treat to see what he comes up with. For *Skin Taker*, I particularly love the imposing bear who heads up Chapter 8, and the horses at Chapter 21, and Wolf at his most magnificent at Chapter 12.

How do the cover designs come about?

While I'm still writing the book, I do a note for John Fordham, the hugely talented designer who created the covers for the original *Wolf Brother* books. My note outlines the plot and mentions any striking features that might spark ideas; sometimes John and I also have a chat on the phone. But the design itself is very much up to him. For some books, such as *Viper's Daughter*, he might come up with several design approaches, and there's then a bit of discussion between me, John, and the publishers, to decide which works best. With *Skin Taker*, though, John pretty much produced the design you see on the cover straight off, and everyone loved it. After that there wasn't a great deal to do other than intensify the colours and make it even more beautiful. I think it's one of his best.

The natural world, and the characters' connection with it, are hugely important in *Skin Taker* – and in all the *Wolf Brother* books. Do you feel strongly about sharing this message with young people, especially now?

I never write with a message. That's probably because when I was a child, I hated books that tried to preach to me. I still do. I write these stories to entertain: to give readers an exciting, immersive, moving experience. Having said that, as Torak and Renn are hunter-gatherers, they are obviously more in tune with nature than we are, because they depend on it so directly for survival. By contrast, most of us have a far more distant relationship with nature – which obscures the fact that we depend on it every bit as much as Torak and Renn.

From what readers have told me over the years, they love the "survival" aspects of the stories, and the characters' closeness to nature. So if my books help foster an interest in the natural world, and perhaps a respect for it and a dislike of waste, that's all to the good. And I've been delighted to learn that the stories have even inspired some readers to become biologists, conservationists and ethologists.

The *Wolf Brother* books are enjoyed by readers of all ages: has that surprised you, and why do you think this is?

When I wrote *Wolf Brother*, I thought it would probably appeal mostly to readers aged between about nine and twelve, simply because Torak is twelve summers old when the story begins. So it did initially come as a surprise when I learnt that adults also enjoy the books; the oldest reader I've met was ninety-nine!

Over the years, I've been constantly fascinated by the differences in readers' responses to the stories. Younger readers might simply enjoy being part of an absorbing adventure with Torak, Renn, and especially Wolf. Older ones seem to love spending time with my Stone Age hunter-gatherers; maybe Torak's world provides a refuge from our frenetic 21st century existence. I've also been struck by how many readers of all ages have told me that the books have helped them through times of loneliness or depression. And lots of people have said how much they enjoy experiencing parts of the stories from Wolf's point of view, through his eyes and ears and nose. So I suppose there's something for everyone – although I didn't realise it when I began writing *Wolf Brother*. I simply wanted to write a thumping good story in a setting I really cared about.

Finally, can you give us any hints about what happens in *Wolfbane*?

I'd better avoid spoilers, so I think all I can say is that Wolf is on the run from an ice demon who wants to eat his souls – so Torak and Renn must find their pack-brother before the demon can reach him. As the title suggests, this final story is focussed on Wolf, and he's in mortal peril. I think readers will find it's a fitting finale for the series.

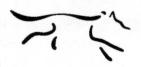

You can enjoy *Viper's Daughter* and
Skin Taker in audio, read by
Sir Ian McKellen